Breathe

Elena Dillon

Rachel,

Enjoy!

Elena Dillon

Dedication

To Kevin, who proved that the prince really can show up
even if the horse is made of steel...

Chapter 1

Most days I can almost forget someone murdered my sister. I try to go through every day like a normal sixteen-year-old. I can eat breakfast, go to school, do homework, but then something will remind me that my family will never be the same. I'll see my mom looking out the kitchen window—she has this blank look and her clothes are hanging on her. I worry she doesn't eat enough to stay alive. Or I catch a glimpse of the picture on the coffee table we took three Halloweens ago, when Daisy and I dressed up like crayons, and Caedan and Lily were Skittles. It seems like a long time ago, and then, again, I remember it like it just happened.

We finally moved two weeks ago. Mom decided we couldn't continue to live in Burbank. Besides the obvious reason that Daisy's murderer was never caught, someone was always staring at us with that look that said, "Isn't it so sad what happened to the Rourke family?" But you know in their hearts they are thinking how glad they are it didn't happen to them. It's obvious they're thinking my mom must have done something wrong. She wasn't a good enough parent, didn't supervise Daisy enough, didn't call the police soon enough. They wanted to believe the murder of a teenage girl happened for a reason and they could avoid it, if they just did everything right. The thing is, I think the exact opposite is probably true.

So, three months ago, we had a family meeting. We got out a map of the United States and each chose a city and state. Mom and I did research on ours, Caedan picked his based on name only, and Lily did the spin-around-and-wherever-your-finger-lands routine. Thankfully, we pulled mine out of the hat. I don't know how I would have felt living in Smackover, Arkansas. Caedan thought it was hilarious. He is so twelve.

Tonight, my mom drove us all to Wal-Mart in our new town of Lafayette, Louisiana. School supplies were the one thing we hadn't shopped for in the last two weeks, and school was starting tomorrow.

"Jas, take your brother and sister to the school supplies, while I go grab stuff for lunches this week, will you, hon?" my mom asked, as she walked away without waiting for my reply.

"I was going to—" I clamped my mouth shut. She didn't even hear me.

I was stuck with this life now. I love my brother and sister, but I hadn't always been the oldest and in charge of herding them. These are the times Daisy's absence hits home the most with me. She had been good with them. I used to slip into the background. Do my own thing. Sneak off to the books and browse, while she did her Junior Mommy act. I'm less patient and easily irritated. I'm angry at Daisy for leaving me here with this mess. I don't want to be the responsible one. I want my life back. I just inherited her spot and, honestly, I don't want it. Not that anything is going to change it now.

"I want to get all matching Justin Bieber school supplies," Lily decided, as we found the school supplies section. The place was crawling with kids and parents getting all their last-minute items. I thought we would be lucky to find filler paper and some pencils, as picked over as it all seemed.

Caedan was pushing the cart around the corners and down the aisles with the precision of a NASCAR driver on Sunday. He knew that one incident, and his driving privileges would be revoked. I was trying to find Justin Bieber anything, as Caedan turned onto the next aisle. Suddenly, I heard a crash and a loud *oomph* as I rushed around the other side.

"Caedan!" I shouted.

"Jas, I'm sorry I didn't know he was there. It was an accident," he pleaded.

"So sorry," I mumbled to the man pushing the other cart. He shot me a look and moved past us. "That's it! I'm driving." But when I looked down at Lily, who had been walking next to Caedan, her eyes were big and full of tears.

"My Justin shirt!" she cried out. I looked down, and in the collision her purple slushy had spilled all over her shirt.

"Don't be such a baby! It is just a shirt," Caedan told her with all the sensitivity of a pre-teenage boy.

"Shut up, Caedan. I hate you." Lily shoved him in the chest.

"Purple is not your color, Lils." He was looking at his twin with pure disgust.

People next to us were starting to stare. I could feel the blood rushing to my face. Why did anyone have children anyway? They were cretins. By this time Lily was starting to melt down.

"Okay, okay, we are going to fix it," I hurriedly told her. Lily had always been emotional, but since Daisy's murder she was hypersensitive to anything upsetting her world, and Justin Bieber was her world.

Into this chaos, my mother arrived. In the past, she could handle these situations quietly and easily. The twins fighting, or Daisy and I arguing over the mess in our room, would not even get us a raised voice. She was an RN for geriatric patients, and she was used to calming situations and peacemaking. Since Daisy's death, even simple sibling arguments seemed overwhelming for her.

"What is going on?" she said between clenched teeth. Lily chose this moment to burst into full tears, while Caedan started protesting about it not being his fault and how mean I was not to let him drive. "I guess it's too much to ask for you to get one thing done for me without any uproar," my mother remarked to me sarcastically. "Jasmine..." The use of my full name was never a good sign. "Go to the car and get your sister her sweatshirt, while I bring her to the bathroom to get her cleaned up." She looked at my brother with narrowed eyes. "You will stand outside the ladies room door with the cart, quietly, while I handle the mess *you* made. And I don't want to hear another word from you while we are in this store. Are we clear?"

I made a face at Caedan behind my mother's back before I whipped around and stomped off to the car. Why was his obnoxious behavior my fault again? Whatever. Being the oldest really was the worst.

As I reached the electronic sliding doors to the outside, I slowed down and caught my breath. It had gotten dark since we had been in the store. After Daisy's murder I had found myself starting to get anxious in particular situations. Outside in the dark could be a problem, sometimes escalating to panic attacks. I tried to keep these little incidents from my mom. She was definitely starting to pay more attention these days.

I scanned the parking lot quickly to find the car. My breath started to come in short gasps. The car was halfway down an aisle, three rows over... and not under a streetlight. Damn! I grabbed my keys out of my purse and stepped into the lot. I would just hurry. I was being ridiculous. This was Lafayette, not Los Angeles. I had nothing to worry about here—lots of miles between us and *him*.

When I was three feet from our car, "Hey there," a male voice said from behind me. I jumped and squealed at the same time. I turned around fast with my pepper spray out. Thankfully, I noticed, before I sprayed, that the nozzle was pointed at me.

"Hey, hey, sorry. I just, um… saw you drop something… um… here." A tall brown-haired boy around my age was holding my mother's list of school supplies. He kept moving toward me. "I didn't mean to scare you."

I kept backing up until my rear end hit the end of our car. "Okay. I, uh…" I said weakly. All of a sudden there was a loud buzzing in my ears, and the world started to tilt.

"Whoa." I heard as everything went black.

I could hear voices around me as I started to wake up.

"Hey, Sleeping Beauty. No time for a nap," a deep, soothing voice said quietly in my ear. "Trenton, what did you do to her? She fainted dead away."

I became aware that I wasn't on the ground, like when I normally wake up from a faint. Since this had happened more than a few times in my teenage life, I found that odd. Due to some hormonal upheaval or whatever, since I hit puberty, fainting had become a fairly common part of my life. But right now, I felt warm, surrounded by the most amazing smell. I was not on the ground with a goose egg on my head as usual. I opened my eyes and saw the most handsome face I'd ever seen. I thought I must still be passed out and was dreaming.

"I was just trying to give her back the paper she dropped, and she acted like I was gonna attack her or somethin'. I don't know why she fainted. I didn't touch her—I swear. Why would that happen? I can't believe you caught her. That was awesome! Is she okay? Do you think there is something wrong with her?" The grating voice kept on until…

"Trenton, shut up," the dream said, still looking into my eyes. I tried to shake my head to wake up and realized I was cradled against his chest like he had swept me up in his arms.

5

Not a dream then. Crap. I became instantly mortified. "I, uh… Can you put me down? Please? I'm so sorry. I didn't mean to faint." Duh.

"Well, I guess, if you really want me to," Dream Guy said as he lowered my feet to the ground.

I couldn't believe he had been holding me while I was passed out. It's not like I'm so heavy. I'm actually kind of skinny, but I'm five foot nine, and he was holding me in the air like I weighed less than a bag of groceries. Time to make a graceful exit. Or any kind of exit. I probably wouldn't be able to accomplish graceful. Who was I kidding?

"Do you normally *mean* to faint?" he asked.

"Um, no. Thanks for catching me. I really have to go," I babbled, while I searched for my keys.

"Here," he said, as he carefully handed me the keys.

"Thanks," I said, as I opened the car and grabbed Lily's sweatshirt.

"Maybe you should—" he started to say, but I interrupted.

"I'm fine, really. Thanks again." I shut and locked the door. They were both standing there looking at me like I was nuts. Well, I guess they weren't far off. This had to be the most ridiculous moment of my life. My face felt like it was burning. I meet the cutest guy ever and what do I do? Faint. Like an idiot. I shouldn't be shocked.

I gave them a little wave as I ran/walked back to the store. I concentrated on getting inside without looking back. If this day was any indication as to how my life in Lafayette was going to go, I should have closed my eyes and pointed.

Chapter 2

The first day at school was more chaotic than I expected. Deciding on an outfit took forever. I didn't know what these kids dressed like. My entire closet was now strewn across my room. I had thought I had my outfit chosen already, but when I put it on this morning I hated it. I finally decided on my newest jeans and a tee I had gotten from Urban Outfitters before we moved. I hoped my California clothes wouldn't look completely out of place here.

Next was hair. Should I put it up or leave it down? I had a lot of hair. It was going to be hot. Unfortunately, when I put all that blond hair up in a ponytail, I looked twelve. Down, it is. All the choices I had to make seemed ten times harder now than they would have been before. That's one of the things I hated about my life now. Someone else made this choice to upend my family, and we all just had to deal with it.

Even getting to school was an issue. My mom had to work. We only had one car, so the bus was a necessary evil. I had to get the twins ready and out the door, since my mom had to work a twelve-hour seven-to-seven shift at the hospital. My bus was crowded and loud, of course, so I just stuck my headphones in my ears and looked out the window. If people wondered who the new girl was, I didn't know about it. I did my best to be unobtrusive.

I went to the office to get my schedule and a map. It looked like I wasn't the only new person to the school, and for that I could be grateful. The school was pretty huge, but I found my morning classes without too much difficulty. I spent the morning trying to get an idea about what the other kids were like and figuring out how to get around without looking like a complete dork. I hadn't really spoken to anyone yet. I'm not super shy, but I am not a really outgoing person, either. Life had been easier with Daisy. Since she was older, she had blazed the trail for me throughout my life. She had been popular and outgoing. She had also been beautiful—black hair and blue eyes. "Black Irish" my dad called her. The exact opposite of me. She was petite, while I was just another tall blonde in a sea of green-eyed blondes in California. Everyone had loved Daisy. I never noticed how easy that made things, until she was gone. Since Daisy was already popular, that made it easy for me at the beginning of high school. I already had the "in." After her murder, I didn't much care about school or friends or sports. All the things that had been so important in my life seemed to fade away with the loss of my sister.

The classes so far had gone pretty well. I had taken mostly AP since it was my all-important junior year. It didn't seem like they were going to be harder than I expected, so that was a relief. I made it to noon without incident, but when I reached the quad where everyone ate lunch, I had the age-old question: Where do I sit? I decided to take my time and check out the situation. I wasn't sure how I was going to fit in here. Would these kids accept me when I obviously didn't come from the South? I was pretty sure I stood out like a sore thumb. Just my height made it hard to blend in. Everyone here had a pretty thick accent, so if I spoke at all it was going to be clear I wasn't a local.

I'd brought an apple from home, so I decided to make my way to a bench and survey the crowd. There was the typical cliquishness, and it was surprisingly easy to differentiate between the groups. The obviously popular athlete/cheerleader group hung out at some benches under a tree. Everyone else divided up into the typical stereotypes: nerds, theater kids, druggies, etc. It was interesting to watch from the outside, for once. I wondered how hard it was going to be to make friends here. So far everyone had been polite, but no one had really made an effort to have a real conversation yet.

I decided to eat my apple and enjoy my umpteenth reading of *Twilight*. The irony was not lost on me. I almost giggled to myself, but not wanting to seem like the crazy new girl, I controlled myself. I was a little weirded out about sitting alone. I tried not to think about the fact that it felt like the whole school was watching how pathetic I was.

"Hey." I heard from right beside me. I only jumped two feet this time as I looked over to see the grating-voiced Trenton of Wal-Mart fame.

"Hello," I responded after I caught my breath. I couldn't believe he was here. I had been so embarrassed last night. Lafayette did have more than one high school. I had hoped that I wouldn't run into either of them again.

"You aren't going to faint, are you?" He was grinning like I had made his day.

"Uh, no." I scowled. He laughed. He was practically bouncing up and down while he straddled the bench.

"I can't believe you go here. I was hoping you weren't just visiting Lafayette. I feel really bad about scaring you. East said I shouldn't sneak up on people, but I really don't think I did that. Did I? Hey, why did you faint?" He certainly could rattle on.

"I just do that sometimes. No big deal," I mumbled.

"Where are you from? You have a funny accent."

I laughed at that. "I don't have an accent—you do."

He was actually kind of cute—or he would be if he didn't talk a hundred miles an hour and ask a million questions. He was tall with light-brown hair and soulful brown eyes. I was pretty sure he was younger than me, so it was more of a little-brother kind of cute.

"You are in Louisiana now, ma'am, and you most definitely have an accent." He smirked. "Where are my manners? My momma would skin me. I didn't even introduce myself," he said, playing up his accent for all it was worth. "I'm Trenton Ward and you are…?"

"My name is Jasmine, but everyone calls me Jas. I'm from LA, you know, Los Angeles. We just moved here two weeks ago," I answered, avoiding my last name, hoping to head off another round of a hundred questions. I knew Daisy's murder had gotten national media attention. I was hoping to put off letting that bit of information out for as long as possible. People immediately treated me differently as soon as they knew who I was—or rather, who Daisy was.

"Wow! LA, huh? Did you live near any movie stars?" he said, hopeful. "You know, like, Megan Fox or Miley?"

I laughed again. "No, sorry."

"Oh bummer." He looked crushed. "So how do you like it here so far?" He perked right back up.

"Good. I haven't really seen much yet. We've been unpacking and getting ready for school," I said noncommittally.

"Well, we're gonna have to fix that. You should come to the pep rally after school on Friday. And the game, of course. I know people say it about Texas, but football is like a religion here too. It's really all there is to do on Friday night. The whole town shows up." He looked at me with a hopeful expression.

"Thanks. I'll try, if my mom isn't working. Do you play?" I asked, trying to seem interested. He was, after all, my only friend so far.

"Of course. I start on JV, but I'm second string varsity. I am only a soph, so… you know…" He looked at me like I would understand the subtleties of high school football politics. I just nodded. "Easton is the starting quarterback, though, so you'll get to see him play."

"Who's that?" I asked.

"Oh, my brother, Easton. You know, he caught you last night?"

I felt myself blushing. Not just blushing. I must have turned red and then three shades of white. "That was your brother? He goes here?" I put my face in my hands. "Are you kidding me?"

He started laughing. "What's the big deal—so you fainted? Happens all the time." He was grinning from ear to ear.

I looked up at him. "This is so not funny. You are talking about the single most embarrassing moment of my life. I was planning on never seeing either of you ever, ever again!"

"Hey, you weren't embarrassed about seein' me again!" he protested.

"Well, you kind of caused the whole thing," I grumbled. All I could think of is, if I had to face Dream Guy again, I would die of an overdose of embarrassment. First day officially ruined.

"Hey, don't worry. He probably forgot by now."

Was he trying to make me feel better or worse? I was trying to figure out a way to change the subject, when the bell rang.

"Hey, want me to walk with you to your next class? What do you have?"

I dug through my bag for my schedule. "French with Paget. Room 203."

"Not too far from my algebra class. Come on, I'll show you." He stood up and led the way. He even bounced when he walked. He reminded me of Tigger. I had to just smile and follow.

I met some girls in French who didn't ask a lot of questions but were friendly and tried to fill me in on where I should and shouldn't hang out. We were supposed to be speaking in French about what we did this summer, but that only lasted about two minutes. Madame knew nobody was ready to go 100 percent into schoolwork yet.

"Don't hang out on the shop side of the school. All the druggies hang out there," informed one girl whose French name was Danielle, but I wasn't sure of her real name. "Was that Trenton Ward who walked you to class?"

"Yeah, he talked to me at lunch. He seems nice?" It came out like a question.

"Oh yeah, he's sweet—a little hyper sometimes, but really nice. And his brother is a hottie."

"Their whole family is gorgeous," added one girl whose French name was Nicole. One of the girls sitting next to Danielle seemed a little more standoffish than the others. When Danielle mentioned Trenton's brother, she got a look on her face that I couldn't figure out. Angry maybe?

"He's not available," she said, glaring at me.

"Well, not as far as you know anyway," Nicole told her with a smirk.

"If not to me, than not to anyone." She turned her glare on Nicole.

I decided not to comment. Were these girls friends or not? I wasn't sure, but I made a mental note to give Angry Girl a lot of space. I did not need any drama.

They went on to gossip about lots of people I didn't know, catching up on summer news. I just sat back and enjoyed being part of a group that didn't look at me with sympathy in their eyes. I missed girlfriends and the mindless chatter that came with them. In Burbank, I had separated myself from everyone by the time we left. I couldn't stand the weight of their pity. I was a little rusty at making conversation and just being one of the girls, but it was coming back to me. I envied these girls their normal lives and their certainty that nothing bad could ever happen.

After school, I supervised the twins' homework, started dinner, and set out my stack of syllabuses for mom to sign. I also checked her schedule on the calendar to see if she was working Friday. It looked like she was off, so I could possibly go to the pep rally and game. The question was: Did I want to? I was still pondering that question when the phone rang. I jumped and my heart started pounding. No one had this number yet. We hadn't given it out. Could my mom be calling? Why would she call the house phone? No panicking. It was either a wrong number or a sales call.

"Hello." Silence. "Hello?"

A muffled whispery voice spoke just one word in a low whisper: "Jasmine." *Click*.

"Hello?" My hands started to shake. What the heck was that? A joke? Maybe. I took a deep breath. I guess my mom could have given the number to someone, but I would be surprised. But how would he know my name? And why did he hang up? Probably just a prank, but now I was kind of freaked out.

After Daisy died, we had to change our number. Three times. There are some really sick people out there. We got all kinds of prank calls at all hours of the day and night. Finally, we got rid of the house phone and kept our cells only. We had to change those too, but only once. We never gave out the number unless it was an emergency. We also got new cell phone numbers as soon as we got to Lafayette. I couldn't believe it was starting up again. We had to have our house phone here because the cell service in this neighborhood was sketchy. Not a very strong signal and unreliable. Surprising in this day and age, but there you go.

After a few calming breaths, I started up the stairs.

"Hey, you guys," I yelled to the twins. "Did you give out the house phone number today?"

As I walked down the hall to their rooms, they both responded, "Why would I do that, Jas?" Caedan said in his most patronizing voice, "I have a cell, duh."

Lily poked her head out of her room. "Did something happen?" she asked, her eyes big.

"No, I was just making sure." I smiled at her. She was a worrier. No need to add anything else to her long list of things to worry about.

Lily looked at me skeptically. "Are you sure?" Lily was very observant, so I had to think quickly.

"Yeah, yeah. Mom just wanted me to remind you, that's all. So when I got that sales call, I realized I forgot to tell you this morning. Dinner in twenty." I swung around quickly and bounded down the stairs, taking a quick detour to check the lock on the front door. When I made my way back to the kitchen, I checked that one too. Fifteen minutes later, my mom got home and we ate together in the kitchen. She was in such a good mood, I decided not to tell her about the phone call. I was probably just overreacting anyway. I needed to get my crazy panic attacks under control.

The next few days held no sightings of Dream Guy. I wasn't sure how I felt about that. He was gorgeous, but I still got a sick feeling in my stomach when I thought about how we met. Sometimes I really wanted to see him again, and other times I was glad I hadn't. He probably didn't even remember me. I don't know why I had spent so much time in the last week thinking about him.

I did, however, see Trenton most days. He had been a big help getting me familiar with how everything worked at the school. I had taken to eating lunch with the girls from French, who turned out to be Julia, Mandy, Raquel, and Lisa. They were actually part of a bigger group made up of all juniors like me. Since I'd always thought making friends and fitting in had been made easier by Daisy, it was a nice change being able to make friends and fit in on my own without any outside influence. Did it make me a bad person that I was excited about doing something without my sister? I had loved her so much, but I wanted to move on in my life. I wished I didn't have to leave her behind. Even making friends here was complicated by my past.

Fortunately, none of the kids asked too much about my past life except the inevitable: Did I know/see/live by any stars? And "Did you live close to the beach?" So funny. They moved on after my mostly "no" answers. I mean, I did see Zac Efron once at Universal Citywalk, but you can't live very long near LA and not see someone famous. I liked most of the girls so far except for the angry girl from French class who turned out to be Lisa. She had seemed to take an instant dislike to me. She had gone out of her way to ignore me and make a show of trying to exclude me from conversations. Thankfully the other girls didn't go along. I just pretended not to notice. This was something I did not miss about girlfriends. She was most definitely a mean girl, and I wanted nothing to do with that. LA was full of mean girls. I knew her type. Yuck.

The pep rally and game was the next day, and I had made tentative plans to go with "the girls," based on mom's approval. It was nice to actually have plans and act like a normal teenager. With the exception of Lisa, I liked hanging out with the girls; they made me laugh. They seemed to get along with each other mostly, and I took that as a good sign. There were some boys that hung out in the group too, but I was still a little ways from being comfortable enough to go beyond "hey" to any of them. I felt like I was waking up from a two-year nap. I was ready to get on with my life. Sad as it was, this was part of the reason we moved. I don't think any of us could have done it if we had stayed in LA.

By Thursday at lunch, the girls were finalizing their ideas for the weekend. I was actually getting excited about being part of it.

"So I think we should make shirts with the numbers of our favorite players on the front. My mom can pick us up the boy V-necks from Wal-Mart," Mandy stated excitedly. "Wouldn't that look so cute? We could totally use the school colors and everything."

"Uhh… I don't even know anyone who plays." This did not seem like a fabulous idea to me. Well, there was Trenton, but I was not going there.

"And isn't that like announcing to the world that you like someone?" Julia reasonably pointed out.

"Well, duh, of course." Mandy rolled her eyes. "Why else would you do it? Boys are clueless. Unless you point it out to them, they don't notice!" Raquel was nodding her head in agreement.

"I'm putting number four on mine," Lisa said.

"You're not going to get anywhere with Easton Ward, Lisa. He already told you he doesn't feel that way about you. You just make yourself look desperate if you put his number on your shirt," Julia told her.

Lisa gave Julia a dirty look. "You don't know. I swear he was staring at me today during break while we were in the quad."

I was surprised to hear he had been there. I hadn't seen him, but then again, there were so many kids smashed together during break, I could have missed him.

"I know you need to give up and move on. He told you he isn't interested." I could tell Julia was irritated with her.

"You don't know anything. You won't even talk to a guy you like. Y'all are ridiculous, and I don't think I want to have friends who don't support me. Y'all are always bringing me down. I am done hanging out with you. I'm out." Lisa glared at us and stomped off.

We all looked at each other. Mandy spoke up first. "Well, that's been a long time coming. What a relief. She was driving me crazy with her Easton Ward obsession."

"He is so polite to her, but you know she has to be driving him nuts," Julia said.

Raquel looked at me and explained. "She's had a crush on him for years, but he has never, ever, been interested. I mean, why would he? He could have anyone he wants. Why would he pick a desperate stalker like her?" Julia and Mandy were nodding.

"Okay, now that we don't have to deal with the crazy, what is everyone putting on their shirts?" Mandy asked.

"I think I'll just put 'Go Lions!' on mine," I decided. I was feeling incredibly awkward after that little incident. I was glad I hadn't mentioned my Wal-Mart moment. Lisa already didn't like me, and she didn't even know about it.

"Well, that makes sense for you, since you don't know anyone well enough yet. But the rest of us have to make a move before all the good ones are gone!" Mandy was pointedly looking at Julia.

"I am not moving anywhere. If he is too clueless to notice, then I'm not interested."

Julia looked to me for confirmation. I had no idea who *he* was, but I slowly nodded my head. Julia was the quieter one of the three, and I thought I would support her if she didn't want to be all out there. Mandy huffed.

"Well, it's easy to see that you two are going to sit on the bench this year. I can't help you if you don't want to be helped!" she complained and moved off to get the other girls on board, with Raquel following behind. Julia looked at me and we both cracked up.

"Well, maybe we should put 'We Love Benchwarmers' on ours?" I told her.

"Or we could put numbers that nobody has and watch them all try to figure it out!" We were laughing so hard, we were crying by now.

"Ohhh, mystery boys! We'll just make ours up!" She decided.

"I'm sure some of the boys on the team are cute." I looked at her sideways.

"I just don't think I want to broadcast that I think that," Julia said, as she tried to catch her breath. "Oh, my stomach hurts," she wailed. The bell rang, and we made our way to class holding our stomachs and giggling.

At the end of my last class, I stayed to ask my calculus teacher to explain a project that I didn't understand. By the time I got out, the halls were pretty empty. I must have been talking to Mr. Evans for longer than I thought. The hallway was already kind of dark where my locker was, and clouds had rolled in. A thundershower was expected by evening. Normally, I would be excited about that. We never got lightning and thunder in LA. Right now, though, it just seemed creepy.

I got to my locker and looked around. How stupid was I that I couldn't even be in the hallway alone? It took me two tries to open the lock because I was a little shaky. At home we all had our own padlocks we used. Here we had to memorize the existing combination that came with the locker. It had taken me all week to get it, but now I was rattled. When I finally flipped open the door and grabbed my bag, something white fell out. I reached down to grab it and started to hyperventilate. A small bunch of daisies mixed in with jasmine and tied with a yellow ribbon were on the ground at my feet.

Fear trickled down my spine. I started to shake. This could not be happening.

"No, no, no!" I backed up fast. I had to get out of there. A loud voice in my head was screaming, *"He's here. Run!"* I took off.

I hit the door at the end of the hall at a dead run, pushed it open with both hands, and turned the corner still sprinting. I hit something solid.

"Oomph!" Arms wrapped around me as we went tumbling to the floor. Full panic set in. I was right. He was here and I was dead. I started screaming.

"Nooo! Let me goooo!"

I had to get away. I was flailing and trying to get up, but the arms were still around my upper body. I was hyperventilating and trying to scream at the same time. A voice broke into the panic.

"Stop, stop. What's wrong? Are you all right?" He grabbed my arms and gave me a little shake. I looked down and realized I was practically lying on top of Dream Guy. He was looking at me like I was a trapped animal and he was trying to decide if I was going to bite him. He put his hands up in front of him as if in surrender.

Terror was still making my heart feel like it was going to pound out of my chest. I pushed off the floor and skidded backward, fast, on my butt, until my back hit the row of lockers behind me. I started looking around frantically to see if anyone else was there and realized, belatedly, that whoever had put that in my locker was long gone by now.

The panic was starting to subside. Relief set in. I put my head in my hands and burst into tears.

"Hey, hey. What's going on? Are you okay?"

I nodded and tried to wipe my face on my sleeve.

He came over and squatted next to me. "Just breathe for a minute."

I shook my head and started to get up. The buzzing in my ears started, so I decided to stay down. I did not want to faint in front of him again. "I got a little spooked, I guess." I sniffled. Was I always going to embarrass myself in front of this guy? Good grief.

"Uh, yeah, I think you did. What happened?"

I was trying to come up with a reasonable response to that without telling him anything I didn't want him to know.

"I, umm… just… you know… got a little creeped out in the hallway by my locker, that's all. It was dark and… " I looked up at him and realized he was even more beautiful than I remembered. He had the darkest hair and the bluest eyes I had ever seen. They were almost purple. He also didn't believe me, I could tell. Dream Guy was no dummy.

"Hmm…" he said as he stood up. "Well, Sleeping Beauty, let's just go and see what there is to be worried about in your locker, hmm?"

"Oh… uh… no, that's okay. I really just got spooked. I can go myself. I'm really sorry I ran into you like that," I babbled. He just looked at me and held out his hand to help me up. I took it. He gave a little pull and just started walking. He kept hold of my hand as I trailed behind him. I tried to pull my hand back, but he had a tight grip and was pulling me forward through the doors and down the hallway to my locker.

"Really, I'm fine. I can go by myself." He didn't slow down.

"Uh-huh." We were almost to my locker, and I could see the door swung open and the flowers on the ground. He stopped and reached down and grabbed the flowers. "This is what happens when someone gives you flowers?" He held them out to me.

I could feel the edge of panic inching its way back in. I started to shake. I took a step back and felt the blood rushing out of my head. "Can you get rid of them? Just throw them away?" I asked. "Please?"

He looked at me for a second. "All right, but I think you need to tell me exactly what is goin' on here. You know, most girls like flowers?" I just took another step back.

He turned and went down the hallway to the trash can and threw them in. Real life was starting to come rushing back. I grabbed my books out of my locker.

As he made his way back, I dug my cell phone out of my purse and saw the time. It was getting late. I needed to check on Caedan and Lily. Fear tried to get another foothold as I pushed myself not to think about where those flowers had come from. Did someone put those in my bag earlier when I wasn't looking, or were they in my locker? I wasn't exactly sure what they fell out of. I stomped down the fear and closed the door on it. I would deal with the flowers later. Right now I had to get home and make sure the twins were all right.

"I have to go. I'm going to miss the bus."

"I can take you home," he offered.

My stomach felt like it hit my feet and bounced back. Drive home with Dream Guy? Safety warnings clanging in my head warred with my heart that was screaming, "Say yes! Say yes!" My heart argued that he had already saved me twice. Pretty sure he wasn't out to kill me.

"You don't even know my name. Are you sure you want to spend time with a freak like me?" I wrinkled my nose.

He laughed. "I am pretty certain you aren't a freak, and I already know your name, Jasmine Rourke." I must have looked surprised and a little wary. "Trenton can't stop talking about you."

Ah, the ever-vocal Trenton. What had he said? Had he told his brother how embarrassed I was about the Wal-Mart incident? I guess it didn't really matter, since the hallway incident would now overtake the Wal-Mart incident in the Embarrassment Hall of Fame. Shame skittered its way into my stomach. I needed to get away from Dream Guy so I could go home and be embarrassed in peace.

"Well, you haven't told me yours, so… I don't know if that is such a good idea." I was still shaky, but I really needed to stop acting like a lunatic around Dream Guy. I closed my locker and started to walk toward the exit to the parking lot. He caught up to me as I got to the doors.

"My name is Easton Ward. We already met at the neighborhood Wal-Mart. You know my brother, so you know I'm not a serial killer. I am a safe, responsible driver with a clean driving record. You'll be safe with me." He grinned.

My heart stuttered at the serial killer reference, but I purposefully ignored it. My heart won the argument.

"I live on Bellevue near University. Is that too far?"

"Nope, just down the road from me. Let's go."

As we came through the doors to the parking lot, I realized the rain had started. It wasn't just sprinkling, like it does this time of year in California; it was pouring. I could hear the thunder in the distance. Easton looked at me.

"We're gonna have to run for it." He grinned and grabbed my hand. We ran all the way to his car laughing like crazy people. I felt like I was ten again, playing in the rain with my friends after school. Some more of the heaviness of the past two years lifted. I could see a future for one brief moment in which not every part of my life was covered by the cloud of Daisy's murder.

As we reached his car, lightning cracked, and I could smell the sulphur. I yelped and he laughed. He opened my car door and ran around to his side and got in. After he closed his door, he shook his head like a dog. I tried to hold my books up to block the water, but it didn't really matter. I was already soaked. "Aargh!" I laughed.

He grinned at me, and I saw the resemblance to Trenton. Except Easton was beautiful, and Trenton was only a shadow of his brother. Maybe in two years Trenton would be amazing too, but right now there was no comparison. He started the car and pulled out of the parking lot.

"So, I've been wondering." He looked over at me. "The other night at Wal-Mart…"

Here we go on the train back to Freakville.

"The fainting, you mean?" He nodded. "It just happens sometimes if I get really startled. No big deal. Unless I hit my head on the way down…" Well, that helped me not to sound like a complete loser. There were two things I did not want to talk about with this guy and this was one of them. I mean, I really didn't want to tell him that my fainting was also related to my menstrual cycle, blood loss, and anemia. Wouldn't that put a lovely picture in his head? Time to change the subject. "So, are you going to the pep rally tomorrow?" He looked over at me and smiled like I wasn't fooling him by trying to change the subject.

"Yeah. Well, if I don't, I would get benched, so…"

I nodded. Silence settled over the car, but it wasn't the kind of silence in which no one knows *what* to say. It was the kind where someone is figuring out *how* to say it.

"So, if you faint when you are startled, why didn't you faint by your locker today? Instead, you were running like the Devil hisself was chasin' you."

My skin went cold and then hot. This was my ridiculous life. Here I was with Dream Guy, and I couldn't even enjoy it. If I told him about my sister now, he would just feel sorry for me. Pity is not attractive. He may think I am nuts right now, but the truth would be worse. *Half-truth it is.*

"Um, I think I just got spooked, not startled like when Trenton came up behind me. I watched something scary last night, so…" I had watched the house phone, scared it would ring again. No lie there.

"Oh, huh." He looked out the windshield and seemed to be deciding something. The weirdest part of this whole wet car ride was that I didn't want it to end, and I couldn't wait to get out of the car. "So what was up with the flowers?"

And there it was. The big question I didn't know how to half-truth my way out of. I needed to be careful here. I felt this weird need to spill my guts to him. Something about him made me want to just crawl in his lap and tell him everything about my life. If I did that, though, he would never look at me the same way. I wasn't sure why he wanted to know, but it wasn't worth the risk.

"Oh my gosh, I have to call the twins. I'm sorry. I'm totally late, and I need to be sure they got home okay."

I rummaged around in my bag for my phone again. Now that I was thinking about it, I really did need to make sure they were all right. I checked my phone. No missed calls. I speed-dialed Lily. Straight to voice mail. Wait. What? I took a breath and hit the number three again. Voice mail. If she'd let her phone battery die, I was going to let her have it. I told myself not to panic. I pushed four. One ring. Two rings.

"S'up?" Caedan popped his *p*.

"Where's Lily?" I barked.

"Downstairs doing homework and being an overachiever. She probably asked for extra work."

"Why is her phone off? You guys are supposed to keep them on, charged, and with you all the time. Even in the house, Caedan."

"Well, I have mine, don't I? Brainiac got hers broken when some doofus threw her backpack and her phone got smashed in the front pocket. Mom's gonna be pissed!"

"Don't say pissed. Is she okay?" This was why I always called Lily first.

"Looks fine to me." He was so not helpful.

"Never mind, I'll talk to her. I'm on my way home."

"Whatever," he grumbled.

"Love you."

"Love you too, freak." *Click*. One improvement in our lives since Daisy's murder? We never, ever, hung up the phone or said good-bye without saying I love you. Even when we were mad.

I sat back in my seat and sighed. "Ugh. Sorry. You gotta love twelve-year-old boys."

Easton laughed. "Yeah, little brothers are a challenge. Trenton is like a puppy on steroids. He goes one hundred miles an hour forever, and then all of a sudden he'll just pass out and sleep like the dead. It's all or nothing with him."

I grinned. "I can totally see the puppy thing. He's very energetic." We were turning onto my street. I pointed out the house. When we stopped in front, I saw the drapes in the front window twitch. Great.

"Thanks for the ride."

As I went to open the car door, he gave me a look and said, "Wait." He jumped out of the car and came around to my side. By the time he got to my door he had his jacket off. He opened my door, saying, "Sorry, I forgot my umbrella. Here." He held out his hand to help me out of the car and held the jacket over my head.

"You don't have to walk me, I can just make a run for it." It felt so awkward having him open my door and protect me from the rain. I was used to doing things for myself.

"Ma'am you are in the South now, and a gentleman walks a lady to her door." He grinned.

"I have noticed a strange tendency towards politeness since I've been here." We walked hunched under his jacket.

As we stepped up onto the porch, he continued to hold the jacket over our heads, and it seemed like we were in our own little bubble.

"Thanks for the ride and soft landing." I looked up directly into his eyes and lost the ability for coherent thought.

He grinned down at me. "Absolutely my pleasure, Jasmine. No more scary movies for you. I may not be there to catch you the next time." He winked at me and walked back to his car. Holy Cow, was I in trouble.

Chapter 3

As soon as I got inside, the interrogation began.

"Who was that boy, Jas?" Lily asked, her eyes narrowed. "You are not supposed to get rides from strangers. You know better!" She was practically hyperventilating. Her breath was coming out in bursts, and she was shaking.

"Lily, it's fine. I know him from school. I missed the bus, and he offered to give me a ride. He is not a stranger. *Really*." I tried to calm her. I gave her a hug. She wiggled out.

"No, Jas, you only just started school, so how well can you know him? He could still be dangerous. What are you thinking?"

Which one of us was the oldest here? Time to reassert some authority. "Lily, cut it out. You are being completely ridiculous. You don't need to worry about it. And what about your phone? What happened at school?" Apparently, not the reaction she was looking for. Next stop, Krakatoa.

"If you aren't going to tell me, I don't have to tell you anything. You don't even care about me or anybody but yourself. He could be really bad, and you wouldn't even know it. I am telling Mom, and you are gonna be grounded! See if I care how *you* feel, Jas!" She ran up the stairs, wailing as she went. *Wait for it. And…* the door slam. Crap. I followed slowly. Of course, the next bright spot to my day popped his head out the door across the hall.

"You're soooo busted!" I got the grin and another door slam.

Well, I was pretty sure that even if I talked Lily out of outing me, Caedan would do it just for the entertainment value. So I was going to have to head my mom off at the pass. But before that, I had to do some damage control.

I knocked softly on the door and opened it. Lily was lying on her bed sobbing.

"Lily." I sat down next to her and rubbed her back. "I'm sorry I worried you." As I sat there rubbing for a few minutes, the crying started to subside a little. "I really do know him from school. I know his brother too." We had moved on to the sniffles. "You know what else? The reason I don't think he is a bad guy?"

A small muffled "why?" could be heard from the direction of the pillow.

"He is kind of a captain on the football team." I saw one eye peek out from the pillow.

"Football players can be creeps too, Jas." But she looked a little appeased.

"Well, I'm pretty sure if he was, he wouldn't have caught me when I fainted in the parking lot of Wal-Mart the other night." Lily sat up. I looked at her out of the corner of my eye.

"No way. You fainted?"

"Yup. I woke up, and he had caught me before I hit the ground and cracked my head open. He's really nice, Lily. His brother is really nice too. His brother is really funny. He reminds me of Tigger. He bounces all the time and never stops talking." Lily giggled. Time for some straight talk. I looked her right in the eye.

"Lils, not every boy is a creep. I'm really careful. Other people say how nice Easton and his brother, Trenton, are. I would never get in a car with someone I didn't know or wasn't sure was nice. I wouldn't take a chance like that. Not ever." The sniffles were back, but not as serious. Disaster averted.

"I was just so worried when I saw you with that boy. I thought maybe you weren't thinking, just because he was cute. I think Daisy did that. I think she maybe thought he was cute, and that's why she went with him." She looked up at me with her big blue eyes and her lip trembling. She really looked so much like Daisy. I was starting to feel guilty for worrying her. I sucked at this. I was never going to be the sister to her that Daisy had been. I wasn't going to measure up, ever—but I had to try.

"Lils, Daisy didn't get in the car with him because he was cute. She must have been forced. She wasn't stupid. She wouldn't have done that. He was an evil man, and we really don't know exactly what happened. Don't start guessing. You know Daisy wouldn't have left us on purpose, right?" Lily nodded.

We had told her this before, but she still ran a lot of theories around in her head. Not knowing was a problem for her. "You don't have to worry. I'm going to tell Mom about Easton, okay?" That was the part I wasn't sure about. Would she overreact too? This was not good. I was not ready for Mt. St. Rose. Sigh… Wasn't one volcano a day enough?

I spent the rest of the afternoon figuring out the way to tell my mom about my ride home, to get the best reaction. I still had the situation with the flowers haunting my mind, but one thing at a time. I was definitely a compartment girl, and that one was going to stay locked down tight until I saw how my mom dealt with the ride home.

When she arrived, she looked distracted. I got dinner on the table. Before I called the twins, I decided now was the time. Just get it out before Caedan could add his two cents. "I just wanted you to know I got a ride home today.

Don't freak out. It was from a boy from school. He's really nice." I looked at my mom and waited.

"All right." She was putting away the groceries she had brought home. Then she looked up and said, "Can you call the twins for dinner?"

Huh? Well that went exponentially better than expected. "Sure." I ran to the bottom of the stairs and yelled. "Dinner!"

When I came back into the kitchen, my mom was serving the enchiladas I had made earlier. I was still waiting for the other shoe to drop, when the twins came scrambling into the room.

"So how many years are you grounded for, Jas?" Caedan smirked.

I smirked back. "I'm not." I raised my eyebrows at him. Take that in, Son! I took my little wars with Caedan seriously. Left undefended, these things could get out of hand. You could never let him think he had the upper hand. He would make you miserable, and there would be no end to the torment. There were not many things in my life that gave me joy, but besting my little brother was one.

We had an understanding. Lily was pretty much off limits. She was too sensitive, so it was no fun to spar with her. He, of course, would still give her a hard time, but he was her twin and knew her limits far better than anyone. Caedan and I, we enjoyed our little battles. We gave no quarter and took no prisoners. We loved to find ways to torture each other. *Punk'd* had been our favorite show, and before Daisy died we had come up with some elaborate ways to get each other. It made my mother crazy, but in many ways it made us closer. No one else really understood it. At the end of a good battle, Caedan and I would always end up laughing together like a couple of hyenas.

"Why would Jas be grounded?" my mom asked, perplexed.

"Uh, duh, because she let some random boy *drive* her home?" Caedan pointed out.

"Jasmine and I will be having a discussion about that after dinner, but it does not involve you, Caedan." My mom looked at him pointedly. He was looking down at his plate. When he was sure my mom was looking away, he wiggled his eyebrows and proceeded to stomp on my foot. I reached my hand down to my leg and made an *L* with my thumb and pointer finger.

I knew that was too easy. Was I busted, or was it going to be just a lecture?

Lily spoke up. "Well, Mom, he is the football captain, and he caught Jas when she fainted. I don't think he's a murderer." I smiled at her but cringed inside. I glanced quickly at my mom. Her expression gave nothing away. This is probably not information I would have shared with my mom, but if it improved my case, I guess it didn't matter. I knew Lily was just trying to help.

Lily and I cleared the table, Caedan took out the trash, and we all did the dishes together. Lily regaled us with the story of the bully who flung her backpack and broke her phone. Apparently, before Caedan could even get to him to defend her, Lily had given him a lecture about bullies. How he would grow up to have no friends, no money, and no life if he didn't apologize right now. She had him eating out of the palm of her hand by the end. He apologized, and by the end of the day wrote her a note to tell her how much he liked her.

We laughed, and I realized that Lily had inherited Daisy's charm and sparkling personality, but that the last two years had made it so hard to see because she now lived in fear and worry of what a monster had brought into our lives. And there he was, the ugly specter, back with a vengeance. Even in these happy family moments, he was there, waiting to ruin them.

As we were finishing up my mom asked, "Are you feeling okay, Jas?"

"I'm just a little tired. It's been a long week." I gave her my best smile to try to cover how I was really feeling.

Those flowers had crept into my mind. Who would have put them in my locker? He couldn't possibly be here. We took great pains to leave very little notice of where or when we were going. Did someone here know who we were? Could someone have recognized us and put two and two together? I had that squirmy feeling in my stomach. When I thought about those flowers falling out, I couldn't remember seeing if they fell out of my locker or my bag. I was trying to think if I left my bag sitting anywhere. At lunch it had sat on the table with the pile of other girls' stuff. A lot of people came and went from the table during our lunch break. Anyone could have shoved them in there. I hadn't even looked in my bag after lunch. I just shoved it in my locker and went to my two afternoon classes.

When we had finished the dishes, my mother told the twins to go to their rooms and finish their homework, that she would be up shortly.

"Jas, let's go out on the porch," my mom suggested. No room for argument there. As we stepped outside, the night felt so humid that the air hung on us like we were wearing it. The rain had come and gone and left even more moisture behind, if that was possible. I would definitely need a shower before bed. "Honey, I want you to tell me why you got a ride home from that boy."

That boy. Uh-oh.

"Well, I stayed to ask my calculus teacher about a project we are doing. By the time I got out, I had missed the bus. *Easton* offered me a ride home." I thought by giving him a name she might relax a little.

"You obviously couldn't know him well enough to make a character judgment when you've only been at the school for four days." My mom narrowed her eyes. "And exactly when did you faint so that he caught you?"

This was not really going as I had hoped. Caedan was going to pay. "When we went to Wal-Mart."

"That long ago, and you didn't feel it was important to let me know?"

"Mom, seriously, you were already in such a bad mood. I was fine! His brother came up behind me in the parking lot—"

"What? What kind of creep does that?"

"No, I dropped your list, and he was trying to give it back to me, but I didn't see him and it was dark. I got startled. All of a sudden everything just went black, and I guess Easton caught me, just before I hit the ground." My mom looked at me with suspicion. "Really. They were just trying to help. The girls at school say they come from a nice family, and the brother is really sweet. Like a puppy." I smiled remembering the comparison Easton had made about his brother.

"Does this boy like you?"

"Mom, it's not like that." I rolled my eyes. "It was pouring. He saw that I needed a ride. Please don't freak out!"

"I don't think showing concern for you is freaking out. I believe I have earned the right to be cautious, and I think you should do the same." My mom gave me the laser stare.

"I am cautious. I asked about them after the Wal-Mart thing. Everyone said they're nice. If they were creepers, someone would have said, and I never would have gotten in the car. If you would have rather I walked home in the pouring rain, I'll do that next time!"

"Okay, okay, don't go all crazy teenager on me. I know you're a smart girl. You need to tell me when you faint. We need to communicate about your life. Please don't just shut me out of everything because you think I'll get mad. I know it's been difficult for you, and I promise to attempt to listen without getting angry. We have to stick together, especially now."

Well, at least she was trying to be rational.

"I want to say thank you for taking such good care of the twins this week. I know it's been a little crazy, getting used to the new routine. I know I don't always say it, but you've been a huge help." She reached over and hugged me.

"Thanks." I felt my eyes start to water and blinked the tears back. I really wanted to tell her everything—the real reason I fainted, the phone call, the flowers. But she was smiling and hugging me, and I didn't want to ruin the moment. What if this was another one of those sick people just trying to get a reaction? It would upset and scare her. It was probably nothing. "It's all right, Mom. I want to help." I smiled at her.

We went back inside, and I worked on my homework. I then realized I hadn't asked her about the pep rally tomorrow. I knocked on her bedroom door, softly, in case she was already asleep.

"Come in." She was sitting up in bed reading with Lily curled up next to her and asleep. "Hey, Mom, tomorrow afternoon is the pep rally, and the football game is tomorrow night. Some of the girls in my class asked me to go with them—is it okay? They're making me a shirt and everything tonight." My mom had that look like she really wanted to say no. "Both things are at school, and we're going to Julia's house for dinner after the rally and then straight to the game. Julia can bring me home if you need the car."

She sighed. "Who are these girls?"

We were moving in the right direction.

"They're all juniors like me. We sit together at lunch every day. Julia's dad is a doctor, and her mom has her own clothing store downtown. She said her mom will be home, and she's going to the game too. I guess the whole town goes. Maybe you should come and bring the twins?" I figured if I invited her, she wouldn't think I was trying to hide anything.

"Have you told them who you are?"

I stared at her for a second. "Uh, no. I was thinking I would try not to. At least not right away."

"Jasmine, it's nothing to be ashamed of. You didn't do anything wrong. What if they find out on their own? They might be upset you didn't tell them."

I sighed and looked down. "I just don't want them to look at me the way everyone at home did. For the first time in forever, people don't feel sorry for me. They just want to be my friend."

"It's your call. Please text me Julia's home number when you get to her house after school, and I want a text when you leave for the game. The twins and I will probably come. Can you introduce me to her mom while we're there? I think it is time to start getting to know the people in town."

"Sure, Mom. Thanks."

I walked back down the hall and into my room. I picked up the picture off my nightstand of Daisy and me. We were hugging and laughing. It had been taken during an almost perfect day at the beach the summer right before her murder. I missed her so much it was hard to breathe. What would she say to me right now? I always asked her what she thought. She was the best big sister. She always said I overthought everything. She was probably right, but in this instance there was a lot to think about.

Did I want my mom to go back to being in touch with everything that went on in my life? Before Daisy's murder, she was very involved at school, knew all my friends' parents, and I could never get away with anything. Even though it was a pretty big town, everybody knew everybody. If your parents were involved and helped at school events at all, someone would tell them what was going on with you. If you were doing something wrong, they were happy to rat you out. I think that's the hardest thing for my mom to get over. She'd been a single parent since my dad left when the twins were five. She was a capable and strong woman. She didn't ever do stuff for herself. Her children were her number-one priority. She was at all our important events. I don't know how she did it, but she never missed a game or something important at school. She drove car pools and baked cookies for the bake sale, all while she worked full time as an RN. She communicated with us, our friends, and their parents. She knew what was going on. She was not out

of touch. She did everything she could do. And the worst
had still happened.

At first, Daisy was just missing. The whole
community launched a search. It was all over the news, all
over the country. Flyers, meetings, search and rescue—all of
the stuff you see on the news when a child goes missing. For
weeks we searched and found nothing. I don't remember
much about that time except that I have never been that
scared before or since.

My mom is an expert at hiding how she feels. I know
she was terrified that we wouldn't find Daisy in time, but
you never would have known by watching her. She seemed
in control and confident. I asked her once while it was
happening how she stayed so calm.

"It doesn't do anyone any good to panic, Jas. Get the
job done, panic later. We need to find her. Freaking out is
not going to do that."

For three weeks the search went on. I heard her crying
every night in her room. Each morning, though, she was out
pounding the pavement and doing everything she could to
find my sister.

The day they found her body, the police came to get
my mom and brought her to the site. She left us at home
with family friends. When she came back that day, it was
like someone had sucked out her soul. The body of my
mother was there, but there was no one behind her eyes. Her
worst fears had come true, and she was only a shadow of the
person she had been before.

She explained to us that Daisy had been murdered.
They found her body in the LA Wash, shoved into a trash
bag. Someone had been looking for recyclables and had
found her. She hadn't told me that—I heard it on the news.
It made me sick to think about someone treating my sister
like trash. She was beautiful and amazing. How dare
someone do that to her? Who would do something so
horrible? Whoever he was, he deserved to pay for what he
did. Someone needed to find him and punish him for his

crime. When they found her, I wasn't scared. I was infuriated and filled with a sadness that made my heart feel like it weighed a million pounds. We had a memorial service. It was standing room only. After, we all waited for them to find her murderer. To get what they all called closure. But they never even got close. The police were unable to get anywhere. They went through everything we owned. Questioned us all endlessly, and still no leads.

They knew that, whoever he was, he had stalked her. There was evidence of stuff he had done. Notes, flowers, e-mails, and phone calls. She hadn't told anyone. Not even me. I think maybe she thought it was a secret admirer at first or just some guy at school. That's how he made it seem. Then, one day, she was just gone.

From that point on, our basic needs were met, but anything above and beyond school and meals was too much. My mother went into her shell unable to handle more than the most basic of routines. I had to help out a lot. We went to school and came straight home. No sports, no afterschool activities for any of us. It sounded bad, but in all honesty, none of us were up for anything anyway. My mother and sister were upset and emotional. Caedan and I? We came out the other side angry. I had a lot of fear too, but the anger was bigger. Or so the therapist said. The last couple of months had been an improvement. Once we had decided to move, the change began. We were starting to move on.

I needed to stop thinking about the past today. I needed to unwind. I went into my bathroom and turned the shower on as hot as I could stand it. I stepped in and breathed deep. I had loved my sister so much. She was so full of life. It was hard for me to believe even now that she was gone.

By the time I got out of the shower I was relaxed enough to force myself out of being sad and focus on getting back into normal things, like my Friday night plans. I convinced myself the flowers were some weird way of someone at school welcoming me. They couldn't know about Daisy. I was a long way from Los Angeles. The phone call could have been anyone. I needed to control my imagination and only worry about things like calculus and boys with beautiful violet eyes. And getting back at Caedan…

Chapter 4

Friday started out slow, but picked up speed quickly. All my classes seemed to drag until lunch, and then, in a blink, it was time for the pep rally. Mandy, Raquel, Julia, and I met in the girls' bathroom in the gym to change into our rally shirts. Mine and Julia's just read "Go Lions!" for which I was immensely grateful. I had been worried that they would just pick a number for me.

Julia smiled and winked when she handed me my shirt. "I did ours myself, just in case they got overly enthusiastic."

I smiled back. That was a relief. I wasn't ready to share who I really wanted to put on my shirt. After the drama with Lisa, I wasn't ready to tell anyone how I felt about Easton. The girls had mentioned he wasn't dating, but for all I knew he could have a crazy ex or something. I refused to allow myself to Facebook-stalk him to find out. I just had to wait and see. Being obvious was not my thing. Most of the time, quiet and unobtrusive is what worked for me. I had been the center of some pretty intense attention at one point in my life, and I could do without it. Being that

Easton was a football star and beyond gorgeous, I really wasn't sure I wanted to be at the center of that.

Who was I kidding? I would probably jump at the chance. Ugh! I was sick of being in my own head. It was going to be good just to go have some fun with my new friends.

We headed off to the school gym for the rally. We found some seats on the bleachers. I hadn't been to a pep rally before. I wasn't even sure if my school back home had them. I guess the point was to get everyone excited about the game tonight. Mission accomplished apparently, because everyone in school crammed into these bleachers that normally were packed away against a wall but slid out for basketball or volleyball games. It was ridiculously hot and sticky inside the gym. We were shoved up against each other in a space meant for half the people it was holding. I hoped I didn't have a desperate need to pee anytime soon because there was no way I was getting out of my seat until it was over.

When the band started playing the school fight song, all the cheerleaders ran out yelling and tumbling. Everyone in the gym stood up and screamed and yelled and caused a ruckus. The football players followed at a more dignified pace. Easton looked amazing in his jersey and jeans. They all took their places in the chairs set up on the basketball floor, and the coaches followed, looking serious.

A pastor of a local church opened in prayer. The coaches spoke about how great the team was going to be this year and how we were going to beat whoever it was we were playing tonight. We were treated to a routine by the cheerleaders and the drill team. Lots of hooting and hollering followed. I barely sat in my seat the whole time. The energy in the room was almost tangible. Everyone was so excited. I had never experienced this kind of hype for a sporting event. My ears were ringing from all the yelling. The band music was loud and echoing in the gym.

I was trying to watch the cheerleaders and the drill team do their routines on the gym floor, but I was distracted by the pull to stare at Easton. I felt a constant tugging to find him where he was sitting with all the other football players. The times I gave in were scary and heart pounding. Once, he seemed to be scanning the crowd, and then the next time he was staring right at me. He smiled. I smiled back and looked away quickly. He filled out his jersey better than the other players. Did he even need to wear football pads? Why was I feeling this way about a guy I had just met? I was so stupid. He probably made every girl feel this way. I needed to hold it together. Passing out a second time wouldn't help the situation. Holy cats, he was so beautiful I could barely breathe.

The rest of the pep rally passed in a blur of color and bad band music. The whole while, all I could think of was how gorgeous he was. When it was finally over, it was so crowded we were trying to inch our way out, but it was like swimming upstream. People were elbow to elbow and smashed up against each other. Everyone from the school must have been packed in for the rally. Trenton was right— football was like a religion here. We moved along the bleachers slowly. Everyone was talking at once in excited voices, and the sound was echoing in my head. The girls were trying to talk to me, but I couldn't really hear what they were saying with everyone talking around me. We got separated from each other with all the pushing and shoving to get out.

When I got to the end of the row, I looked up and Easton was standing in front of me. I was instantly a mortified mess. I could feel all the sweat dripping down my back, and I pictured what a disaster I must look like after being squashed in between all these people in the insanely hot gym. He, of course, looked like he just stepped out of an Abercrombie ad. Except he had clothes on.

"Hey," he said with his killer smile.

"Hey," I replied. How original.

"I was wondering… are you going to the game?"

I tried to think, but his gorgeousness was making it difficult. "Um, yeah." Brilliant. I was a brainless idiot. I was sure he wasn't shocked.

"Well, we all usually go to the diner after the game. Would you like to go with me?" He looked at me through the fringe of his hair.

"I… uh… Sure. That would be fun."

His smile got bigger. "Good. It'll take me a little while before I get out of the locker room after the game. Do you mind waiting? I could meet you by the snack shop." I looked at my friends, who were standing behind him. Their mouths were hanging open. I must have been six shades of red.

"That's… uh… great. I'll meet you there."

"See you then, Miss Jasmine. Ladies." He nodded to the girls as he headed toward the boys' locker room. What had just happened? Did he just ask me out? Did I just say yes? I could feel my breath start to come in short, fast gasps. And I'd acted like a dork in front of him again. I couldn't figure out if I was excited or horrified.

In a heartbeat I was surrounded and dragged away by three squealing girls. Mandy, Julia, and Raquel were hustling me out the door to the car, but before we went through I saw Lisa glaring at me from the corner. Crap. Not good. She must have seen him talking to me. Did she know he asked me out? Could she tell? That would be bad. Like I needed more drama right now. I wondered how crazy this girl really was. Before I could dwell on it too much, the girls started with the inquisition.

"Oh. My. Gosh! Did Easton Ward just ask you to the diner after the game?"

"Um… yes?"

Louder squealing.

"How do you know him?"

"He's a senior!"

"He's the quarterback!"

"He doesn't date anyone at school. Ever."

"How did this happen?"

"Tell us everything!" Much more squealing.

Somehow we had made our way to the car, but I wasn't sure how. I was overwhelmed with the rapid-fire questions.

As we got in, Mandy and Julia turned around in the front seats. "This car is not moving until you spill!" Julia demanded.

Ugh. In order for me to tell them what happened, I would have to share my most embarrassing moments. Did I want to do that? I really wanted to have girlfriends again. Maybe it would be all right. I didn't have to tell them anything else yet. They seemed trustworthy, and I could swear them to secrecy and hope they kept it to themselves.

"If I tell you the story, you have to swear not to tell another living soul. The events I am about to share with you are the most embarrassing of my life." I narrowed my eyes at them. "I also expect you all to share equally embarrassing stories with me at some point this evening to make it even. If a word gets out about any of the details of these stories, I'll know where it came from, and I will make it my mission to destroy you." I stared each one of them in the eye. They all stared back solemnly and nodded. "Pinky swear." I stuck out my pinky, and we all linked together and shook.

"Nobody better spit in my car!" Julia shouted.

"No, no spitting! Unnecessary!" I exclaimed. Spitting made me nauseated.

I told them the Wal-Mart story. I explained about my "condition" and why I faint so easily. When I got to the part about Easton catching me, all three girls squealed again and then sighed.

"That is the most romantic thing I have ever heard of happening in real life." Julia sighed again.

"Is that all that happened?" Mandy asked.

"Well, I sort of ran away after he put me down." I smiled sheepishly.

"What? Why?" she demanded.

"I was so embarrassed! I hate fainting. I felt like an idiot!"

"Okay, okay. Go on. Then what?" Raquel asked.

"Well, I saw Trenton the next day at lunch. I think he felt bad, so he walked me to class."

Julia shook her head. "That is so not why he walked you to class!"

I gave her the stink eye. "He's just a kid."

"Uh-huh."

Mandy and Raquel were bouncing in their seats. "Go on, go on!"

I filled them in on the other day in the hallway, but left out that I had been spooked. I didn't want to explain it yet. I was just not ready to see the pity on their faces when I told them who I am. So I just said I knocked him down running for the bus. I was getting good at half-truths. I told them about the run in the rain and the ride home.

I think Mandy was ready to swoon.

"That is amazing! Do you know what this means?" Her eyes were like saucers.

"No, what?" I asked warily. What did I miss?

"You're dating Easton Ward!"

"No, no, no. He asked me to the diner. That doesn't mean we're dating. That's one date. That's it."

Raquel and Mandy exchanged looks.

"What?" I demanded.

"Wellll…" Raquel dragged out. "The diner is where you go when you want to make your relationship public. You don't go there with someone you are just seeing. Guys only take girls there when they are serious. When you go there, everyone will see you together and assume you are dating exclusively." Raquel gave me a sly look. "I think it's interesting that he's taking you there when he has never, ever, taken a girl there before… and there is really no way you would know what it means, but everyone else will," she informed me, all in one breath.

Mandy was nodding, and Julia stared at me wide-eyed. "Wow," she muttered.

I was officially panic-stricken. I was already scared out of my tree about going anywhere alone with him again. I had made an idiot of myself so many times already, I couldn't believe he didn't think I was a complete loser. I also had to figure out a way to go to the diner with him and not have my mom find out. All this added pressure was not helping.

"I think you all are overreacting. I'm sure he doesn't mean it like that. It's probably just because all his friends are going."

They laughed. "Uh, no," Raquel responded. "No way."

Julia finally started the car, and we made our way to her house. She lived in an upscale neighborhood. Even though her house was definitely on the fancy side, it had a very lived-in feel. Cozy and homey. It was one of those houses that had a great room that opened to the kitchen, where everyone hung out and ate popcorn and watched movies together. It was so different from mine. Not because it was fancier and nicer but because it had a lightness that I recognized. I remembered the lightness. There was nothing weighing it down. There was no burden of grief here. My house used to feel like this. It had been gone a long time. I wanted it back, but I wasn't sure if it was possible or how to go about making it happen.

Her mom was really nice. She was bustling around the kitchen fixing dinner for us: Chicken Caesar Salad, homemade crusty bread, and sweet tea. It was wonderful not to have to think about cooking. My mom had been working so much this week, I spent a lot of time in the kitchen at home. I do the majority of the cooking for our family and have since Daisy's murder. I don't mind cooking. I actually like it sometimes, but I was always happy when someone else took care of it. I felt like I was being spoiled.

After dinner, we helped clean up and went upstairs to freshen our look. Quick showers were in order. I hadn't known, but the girls made two sets of rally shirts. Apparently being seen in the same shirts from the rally was bad. Curling and straightening hair, and makeup, needed to be done and we only had a short time. As there was never enough time for four teenage girls to get ready, of course we were late.

Waiting in line to get in, I couldn't believe the crowd. By the time we got through the gate, I felt like I needed another shower. It had not cooled off much from earlier, and the air was still thick with humidity. The lights in the stadium were so bright, it was lit up almost like daytime. It was immense and loud. I could hear the band playing and smell the popcorn. I hadn't gone to many of my high school football games at home. Daisy's murder had happened, and I just never got involved or even cared, so I really couldn't wait to be a part of it all now.

The game hadn't started, but we had to hurry to get to our seats before it began. The other juniors were all in a section together, and we just smushed in with the rest of them. There was more jumping, yelling, and shouting, similar to the pep rally but much louder. I didn't know all the rules, but I could keep up with the game well enough. I spent most of the time following number four, anyway.

We were ahead at halftime. After watching the cheerleaders' halftime routine, we all needed to run to the bathroom. Of course the line for the girls' bathroom was ridiculously long. We spent the time in line talking about the game and what everyone was wearing. The boys all seemed to smirk at us when they came out of their side and saw we were still waiting. So unfair. When I finally got into the stall, my phone vibrated. It was a text. I figured my mom wanted me to introduce her to Julia's mom. When I opened the text, my stomach felt like it hit the ground.

Did you like your flowers? You and I were meant to be together…

My heart started pounding, but I made myself breathe. I dropped my phone. Crap. I tried to pick it up, but my fingers weren't cooperating. The sides of my vision started to go a little dark. Breathe, dammit! I was not going to faint in the bathroom stall over a stupid text. I dropped it again, and the back popped off. It took a little doing to get it back on because my hands were shaking so bad. Once it turned back on, I looked to see who it was from.

Blocked.

Not unexpected. No need to panic. This could be anyone. It could be some weirdo messing with me, even though my number changed. I think people would be shocked to know how easy it is to get someone's cell phone number. Actually, it's rather easy to come by just about anyone's personal information. This we had learned quickly in the months after the murder.

I couldn't respond or track the number, so I was going to ignore it for now. I closed my phone and put it back in my pocket. I made myself breathe slow and steady. I closed my eyes and counted to twenty. I was still not convinced there was a problem. A lot of weird stuff had happened before we left LA. I had learned not to make hard-and-fast decisions in the last couple of years. Thinking about what you do before you do it is better. I probably overanalyzed everything, but better that than being impulsive. I didn't like where impulsive could end up. I took a deep breath. I was still a little shaky, but that would stop soon.

When I left the stall, the girls were waiting for me already. I smiled at them and went to wash my hands. I wasn't going to let them see me have an anxiety attack. I couldn't let fear get the best of me. As we all tromped back to our seats, I was feeling better. Compartments were my friends.

I did get a call from my mom later in the game, but they hadn't come. Lily had a cough, and Mom had thought it better to keep her home. The three of them were having a Scrabble tournament. She had already talked to Julia's mom on the phone, while we were getting ready. It was fine if I wanted to spend the night, but I needed to be home by ten a.m. tomorrow to help around the house with chores. Fortunately, that resolved how I was going to get away with going to the diner with Easton.

It isn't that I didn't want to tell my mom because I thought she would say no. It was really because I didn't know where the whole thing was going. I needed to be able to tell her in a controlled setting and explain what was going on. If I just called and said he wanted to take me to the diner, she'd switch into instant Overprotective Mom mode. Since the girls had said they would go too, I wasn't really going to be out with him without supervision. The girls, of course, wanted to observe the "date" for later consultation. I wasn't sure if having them there would make me more nervous or less. My life was going from uncomplicated to complicated very quickly.

As the game was nearing its conclusion, we were ahead by seven points, so there was still some pressure on. I was screaming myself hoarse. Easton made a long pass, and I held my breath. Our receiver made a beautiful catch and ran it in for a touchdown. Everyone in the crowd went nuts. The kicker made the extra point with less than three seconds left on the clock, and we had our first win of the football season.

I realized, as I was jumping up and down and screaming, that I was starting to feel like a part of something. I was starting to blend and meld into a student of my new high school. It felt really good. If I didn't think about all those compartments that were starting to line up, life was looking pretty good.

Chapter 5

As we moved out of the bleachers, my stomach started to flutter. Everyone was talking about the game, going to the diner, and who was riding with whom. The girls decided to meet me there rather than wait, so I wouldn't be embarrassed—and more importantly for them, they would get a good table to watch the entire "date." Fantastic.

I took my time getting to the snack shop. I knew I would have a bit of a wait with the coach's after-game lecture, and the team's showering and general horsing around because they had won. There was only one person left in the snack shop when I got there. She was a very pretty mom type with long brown hair caught up in a messy bun and a sweet smile.

"Oh, sweetie, we're closed. I'm sorry," she said.

"I'm just waiting for someone. I'm good."

"Oh, all right. I just really need to get this all cleaned up and organized or I'll never get home. It's a nightmare every week. If you don't stay on it, it takes on a life of its own." The woman was bustling around putting things away.

"I could help if you want. I think I'll be waiting awhile," I offered. There were still people milling around, but I liked the idea of being inside the snack shop doing something rather than being outside looking around like a loser. Busy sounded better.

"That would be great. What's your name, sweetie? You look so familiar."

Uh-oh. "Uh, everyone calls me Jas."

"Is that short for somethin', darlin'?"

"Yes, it's Jasmine."

"Well, that is a lovely name. I'm Mrs. Sullivan. I am part of the Athletic Booster Committee. We raise money for the athletics at our school. The lady that had signed up to help me—well, her son was the one who was injured tonight. Did you see that?" I nodded. "They think he might have broken an arm. I told her to go ahead and not to worry; I would take care of everything, but I sure am glad you came along. I would've been here all night!"

She let me in the back of the snack shop and handed me an apron. Then she put me to work putting away the candy that was still unsold and organizing it by each kind. She was cleaning out Crock-pots and putting away all the paper products. She rattled on about the messy teenagers who worked there and about the game. I was glad to have something to do. I didn't have to say much, just nodded or agreed in the right places.

"Sweetie, are you sure we haven't met? I almost never forget a face, and I can't figure out where I have seen you before."

Not good. "I moved here three weeks ago, so unless I saw you at Wal-Mart, I don't think so." I smiled.

"Well, that could be it. It'll come to me anyway, as soon as I'm not thinking of it."

We worked in a companionable silence for a while and then she asked, "Who are you waitin' for, sweetie? It's startin' to get late."

The back door to the snack shop opened and I heard, "Well, now, she is waiting for me, Aunt Bellie. Are you working her to the bone back here?" And there he was. His hair was still damp from the shower. He was gorgeous and I couldn't breathe. He smiled at the woman and she had a big grin.

"Oh really? Well, I think I should warn her about spending any time with a Ward boy. You know, my sister got involved with one of them a while back and look what happened!"

Easton grabbed her around her waist and picked her up. "I hear she got herself in trouble and ended up having to marry that wild man," he said as he swung her around.

She laughed. "You heard right. And she ended up with a couple of boys just like him. What's a girl to do?" She grinned. "Now put me down, you heathen! This girl has been waitin' on you. And you better be treatin' her right, or else."

He gave her a big smooch on the cheek and set her down laughing. "Don't worry, Aunt Bellie, my momma raised me right." He winked at her.

She swatted him with a dish towel. "Jasmine, you let me know if he steps a toe outta line. You have to watch him. He's a charmer, just like his daddy."

I, of course, hadn't met his dad, but wouldn't be surprised if the charm and good looks were genetic. "Oh, I will, don't worry. It was nice meeting you."

"You too, sweetie. Thanks for all the help."

Easton grabbed my hand and led me out of the snack shop.

"Your aunt's really great," I told him.

"Yeah. My mom has three sisters and she's my favorite. They are all pretty great, but she's my Cousin Chase's mom. Chase and I are the same age. We practically lived at each other's houses growing up. She's like my second mom. So I spent the most time with their family and the same went for him. You'll meet him at the diner."

I nodded. I wondered what it must have been like, having such a big family.

"Why do you call her Aunt Bellie?"

50

He laughed. "Her name is Annabelle, but the Bellie part came when she was pregnant with my cousin Finn. We were pretty little. Her belly got really big, so instead of calling her Aunt Annabelle, I nicknamed her Aunt Bellie. It kind of stuck. Now all the cousins call her that. What can I say? She loves me." He shrugged. He was adorable.

As we walked out of the stadium, I thought how different it looked from just a short while before. It was so quiet, almost creepy. As we approached the parking lot, I realized that when I was with Easton I didn't feel panicky in the dark. Weird. I always felt like that, even with my mom.

"Did you have fun at the game?" he asked.

I smiled. "It was really great, especially because we won."

"Yeah, that does usually make it more fun." He pulled my hand so I was closer to him, our shoulders brushing as we walked.

I wanted to tell him how great he did, but I didn't want to sound like a gushing idiot. "Did you have fun?" I asked.

"Well, now... I guess I did," he said as he opened my door. I was starting to get used to all these manners. He went around to his side and got in.

"You did really well. That last pass was amazing." Next stop: fan-girliness.

"Well, the team makes it easy." He never seemed full of himself, even though he easily could be.

We got to the diner in minutes. It was only a few blocks away, and it was packed. I could feel my heart start to speed up. For normal people, this kind of thing would probably not be a problem. For me, however, it presented more than one. I had actually never dated. The last two years, when I probably would have been considering it, I wasn't in any state to even think about that. Plus, I never knew what anyone's motives were back home. Pity, notoriety, morbid curiosity—or were they truly interested? There hadn't been anyone who seemed worth figuring that out for. So, honestly, this was my first date, *ever*. And it was with the most popular boy in school—in front of the entire school. No problem. I just hoped I could keep from hyperventilating.

We parked and Easton turned off the car. He looked at me before he went to open the door.

"Ready?"

I nodded.

"You have that same look you had that day by your locker. Are you sure you're okay? We can go somewhere else if you want."

"I'm fine. Let's go," I insisted.

He didn't move. He looked at me, and I knew he was evaluating whether or not to believe me.

"Really. I know it's going to be a little overwhelming, but it's all right. There are just a lot of people. I don't really like being stared at," I said sheepishly.

"Jasmine, you're a gorgeous girl. You're going to have to get used to the staring someday."

I glared at him. "I know they must check your eyesight before football starts, but I'm starting to wonder."

I went to open my car door and he gave me the look. He mumbled under his breath as he got out of the car. I thought he said something about a mirror, but I wasn't sure.

He opened my car door and grabbed my hand as we walked across the parking lot. I got goose bumps. I wasn't really a touchy-feely kind of girl, but I never wanted to let go of his hand. I already liked him so much it was scary. How had this happened so fast? He was rubbing his thumb up and down the back of my hand as we walked. I felt like all the nerves in my body were centered in my hand at this moment.

When we got inside, he didn't wait for someone to seat us but seemed to be making a beeline for a booth that had another couple in it. There was lots of hooting and hollering as we walked in. I felt like ducking. I saw the girls in the corner and half waved, not wanting to draw to attention to myself. I sort of kept my eyes on his back and just followed. He stopped in front of the booth, put his hand on my elbow, and helped me in. I scooted across the seat, and he plopped down next to me.

"My man, you're late. We're celebrating." The blond boy across from Easton slapped him on the shoulder.

"Chase, this is Jasmine. Jasmine, this is my cousin and favorite receiver, Chase." He stuck his hand out and I shook it. He actually didn't look at all like Easton. He was very good-looking, but he was blond with a different shade of blue eyes. He did, however, have the same grin.

"Lovely to meet you, Miss Jasmine. This is the love of my life, Whitney."

I recognized her from school. Whitney was beautiful. She had dark-brown hair, brown eyes, and bowtie lips. She smiled and stuck her hand out.

"I believe we have English together. So nice to meet you, Jasmine." Her voice was quiet but lilting, and with her accent, I could have listened to her all day.

"Nice to meet you both." We chatted a bit about California and the differences between the schools and weather. The waitress took our order quickly, looking like she couldn't wait for us all to leave. Easton and I decided to share a hot fudge sundae.

I was starting to relax, when a bunch of football players jostled up to our table. They were shoving each other and being loud. One of the players decided to be the spokesperson for the group.

"Who's the girl, East?" Some catcalling from the group ensued.

"Jessie, this is Jasmine." Easton narrowed his eyes at them and continued. "Jasmine, this is Jessie and the whole offensive line. Please forgive them their poor manners. Apparently winning has gone to their heads." More catcalling and shoving.

"Ohhh, Jasmine. Like the flower. Nice to meet you, flower girl."

Chase spoke up. "Obviously you losers were unable to get dates for the evening. No one is shocked, by the way. We would appreciate you not ruining ours. You also forget that Easton and I are captains of the team and therefore in charge of deciding exactly what conditioning y'all will be doing next week at practice. I'm sure you won't be interrupting again?"

There was grumbling and mumbling and lots of pushing and shoving up the aisle. Easton and Chase executed a casual fist bump and carried on the conversation as if the interruption had never happened. I looked at Whitney, and she just rolled her eyes as if this kind of thing came with the territory.

We finished our desserts. Then Whitney reminded Chase that her curfew was not too far off. Chase leaned in and looked at me.

"We need to head out. Can't get on Whitney's dad's bad side. He's the principal." He wiggled his eyebrows.

I giggled. "Oh my gosh!"

Chase had a long-suffering look. "Tell me about it. I must love her."

Whitney shook her head and shoved him to get out of the booth. "Come on, Trouble. Let's go." They walked out and I looked at the time. It was getting late. Julia needed to be in soon too.

"What time do you have to be home?" he asked.

"I'm not going home. I am spending the night at Julia's." I pointed to the girls' booth. He nodded. "But Julia needs to be home in half an hour. I don't want to get her in trouble, so…"

Easton smiled easily. "Of course, Jasmine. I will have you to Julia's in plenty of time." We got up from the table after he left enough for the check and a nice tip. I just loved that. If someone was a generous tipper, it seemed to me they had a generous heart. Did this guy have a flaw anywhere?

As we left the diner, I saw that the boys who had come to our table had stopped to squish themselves into the booth with the girls. Mandy and Raquel were laughing and talking, but Julia looked uncomfortable. One of the boys in the booth was sitting next to her, but they didn't seem to be talking.

We got in the car and headed out. Apparently Easton knew where Julia lived, which was a good thing because I realized I didn't. Her older brother, who graduated last year, had played football, so I didn't have to ask Julia for directions. We drove, listening to the radio. I was thankful that Easton didn't seem to expect me to fill the silence. I guess, being a girl, everyone always expects me to chatter nonstop, but I would rather say nothing than something stupid. It was nice to just enjoy his company.

When we pulled up in front of Julia's house, the girls weren't there yet. Rather than make me wait outside by myself, Easton insisted on waiting for them to get there. He turned in his seat to face me.

"So are you ever gonna tell me why those flowers scared you?"

Honestly, I had kind of been waiting for this one all night. I can't say I was surprised, but I still wasn't really ready to answer. "Well, the answer to that is actually not as simple as you might think, and we really don't have time for me to answer it right now." Well, that was true enough. The minute I explained what really scared me about those flowers, there were going to be a lot of questions. And unfortunately, he would probably never feel the same way about me again.

When I was working with his aunt in the snack bar, I realized I needed to come clean—with him, at least. His aunt was one of those people who would figure out who I was, and it probably wouldn't take long. During Daisy's murder investigation and all the TV press conferences when we were trying to find her killer, I was prominently displayed. My mother was basically catatonic directly after my sister's body was found, so I spoke for her a few times. I was pretty direct in speaking to the killer on camera about what I thought of him. The major networks picked it up and ran with it because I was fourteen and well spoken. I guess it moved people, or whatever.

If I knew then that it wouldn't have helped and would lead to my situation being what it is, I wouldn't have done it. Well, I guess that's not true. At the time I would have done anything to catch him. I have never been so angry or scared in my life. I thought catching him would make the pain and fear go away. The reality is, though, nothing would have fixed it. You can't undo death. It wouldn't bring her back. And honestly, once something that bad happens, the certainty that nothing bad will ever happen to you is a thing of the past.

I looked out the window and sighed.

"I know I just made it much more mysterious and shady sounding, but it's true." I turned in my seat to face him.

He shook his head. "Well, that is not at all what I was expecting. You're a fascinating girl, Jasmine Rourke." He smiled. "Give me your phone."

Uh. "Sure." I handed it over. He pushed a bunch of buttons quickly, and I heard a ringing in his pocket. When he took his phone out to look at it, he quickly turned to me.

"Why does your number come up blocked?"

Oh boy. "Um, my mom is a little paranoid. I'll put it in for you." I grabbed his phone and put it in.

Just then, Julia's car flew into the driveway with the windows down and the radio blaring.

"I guess I better go. Thanks for taking me; it was really great."

He nodded and looked serious. "Can I call you later?"

What was he? Nuts?

"Yeah, sure."

He gave me the death glare before he got out, which I interpreted as: open the car door and you will suffer my wrath. He opened my door and started to walk me to the front door, but the girls were all standing in the driveway laughing and talking really loud. So we walked over that way.

"Good evening, ladies." Easton smiled at them. Hi's and heys could be heard all around. "Julia, I will leave Jasmine in your hands. Please take good care of her for me." He winked and walked away.

Good grief, was it possible to die from an overdose of charming hotness?

The girls were giggling as we walked into the house. I texted my mom to tell her I was back at Julia's. We all tromped upstairs like a herd of elephants. We got into our jammies and settled into sleeping bags to rehash the night's events. I realized I was happy. A cute boy liked me, I had friends I really bonded with, and I felt like a regular teenager again. Would that end the minute I told him who I was? I really hoped not. It had been a perfect night so far. Well, almost perfect if I ignored that text—and I intended to. There was nothing I could do about it now. I was more worried about Easton's reaction to my story. I hoped he wouldn't think I was more baggage than I was worth when I told him. I had a knot in my stomach from thinking about it. Would he even want to know me? I guess I would find out soon. I knew he wasn't going to be put off much longer.

I did force the girls to tell me some of their most embarrassing moments while we were settling in for the night. We laughed so loud at one of Mandy's stories that Julia's mom had to come in and hush us. At least we were on even ground now.

An hour and a half later, Julia and I were the only ones still awake, watching the girly movie we had picked out, when my phone pinged. It was a text from Easton.

Are you awake?

I looked at Julia. She was still watching the movie, but she was smiling. I answered.

Yes. Watching a chick flick. U?

I put my phone down. It was just too pathetic to stare at the phone until he answered. I tried to concentrate on the movie. It pinged again in just a matter of seconds.

Thinking about u. Can u talk?

Hmm. Could I talk? I didn't want to take the phone in the bathroom and have him think that I was peeing or something. Besides, if you think people can't hear what you are saying when you're in the bathroom, I'm here to tell you it's probably the easiest room in the house to eavesdrop. Daisy used to talk to boys in the bathroom, and I knew everything she was up to. Well, obviously not everything. So, not the bathroom. Outside?

"Julia?"

She grabbed the remote and paused the movie. "What's up?" She was looking at me expectantly.

"That was Easton texting me. He asked if I could talk, but I don't want to bother you or your family. Do you mind if I go outside? Would your parents mind if I sat by the pool for a few, if I'm quiet?"

"You know he really likes you, right?" she said with a smile.

"I don't know," I told her.

"Jasmine, I know him. He's friends with my brother. He's crazy about you. Go sit on one of the lounge chairs out there. My parents won't care." I thanked her and texted him back that I needed to go outside.

I made sure all the lights were on by the pool, so I could sit out there without hyperventilating. I hoped they didn't disturb anyone, but even with the moon out, it was still pretty dark. Once I got settled on the lounge chair on the far side of the pool, I took a deep breath and pushed Send.

"Hello, gorgeous," he said, answering the phone.

I laughed. "All right, Mr. Charming, you can tone it down now. Your Aunt Bellie was right. I better watch out."

He chuckled and his voice sounded gravelly.

I shivered and told myself it was chilly out here. Right.

"Now don't go putting too much stake in what Aunt Bellie says. She just likes to make trouble for me."

I'm sure she did. "Sounded to me more like a warning for my own good." I probably needed a warning if I was going to keep my head with him and all his hotness.

"Well, I can't see that you would be needin' that. I think it's the other way around. I can't stop thinking about you. Are you ever gonna tell me something about yourself, or are you gonna make me go crazy guessing what makes you tick?"

I sighed. "What do you want to know?" There was a pause. I knew what was coming.

"I know you're going to think I'm a jerk to keep asking, but you have me worryin' about what could have freaked you out that bad. I saw your face before you ran into me, and you were terrified. My imagination is good, but I can't figure it out. But I don't want you to think that's all I'm interested in. You're great, and I really love spending time with you. It worries me to think there is something so wrong in your life."

Well, this would be interesting. I'd never had to tell anyone before. Everyone back home already just knew. No more half truths. Time to come clean.

"Two years ago my sister was murdered by a serial killer. He was never caught. Her name was Daisy Rourke."

I heard him suck in his breath. "You're *that* Jasmine?" The light comes on and…

"Yup." Cue the pity. *Please God, don't let him feel sorry for me.*

"And the flowers?"

Huh. "Daisies and jasmine wrapped up in a yellow ribbon. I got freaked out because I didn't think anyone here knew who I was. Obviously someone does and thinks they're funny." Why was he not doing the sympathy thing?

"Shouldn't you call the police about the flowers?"

Interesting.

"No. It's nothing to worry about. After it happened, people did weird stuff like that. They think they're just playing a prank or whatever." I tried to sound casual.

There was a pause. I decided to give him a way out. Obviously, it was more than he signed up for.

"You can gracefully bow out now if you want. I totally get it. Knowing me comes with some unwanted baggage. I wouldn't want to get tangled up with me." I held my breath. Why was it that when everything seemed to be going so well I felt like the bottom was going to drop out? I didn't want this life. I hadn't asked for it, and all this baggage doesn't even belong to me. Was this the last time I would talk to him on the phone?

There was a sigh on the other end of the line. "Jasmine, I do believe you've just insulted me. Do you really think I wouldn't want to be around you because of that psycho? You're amazing. I remember seeing you on TV. You were so brave for fourteen. I would have been curled up in a corner if something like that happened to Trenton. I can't believe that was you. I'm proud to know you."

Wow, not the reaction I was expecting. He really didn't want to run away now? I was shocked and grateful. Why did this amazing guy want to be around me? I wished he was here in person.

As I looked out over the pool, I thought back to standing in front of all those microphones. It seemed like yesterday and a long time ago—all at the same time.

"Well, don't believe everything you see on TV. I was really scared. But I guess I was more angry than anything. It was stupid. It didn't do any good. They didn't catch him, and all people think of when they see me is 'That poor girl's sister was murdered.'" Too much information. I should just shut up now.

"Jasmine? That may have been what they were thinking back home when you were fourteen, but that is *not* what they're thinking now."

I laughed. "Yeah, now they are just wondering *why* I'm such a freak." I could hear him roll over in his bed.

"Well, not if they're like me. If they're like me, they're thinking 'How do I get the nerve to talk to that gorgeous girl?' I was just lucky and you fell at my feet before I could decide."

I was shocked. I couldn't believe he didn't think I was pathetic or a freak. Or just a pathetic freak. How was that possible? He was Dream Guy. "I'm sure you have girls falling at your feet all the time."

He chuckled. "No, you were definitely the first, and the first girl to tackle me to the ground, by the way. If that little bit of information gets out, I can kiss my college football career good-bye."

I smiled. How did he do that? I think I had smiled more in the last two days than I had in the last year. "Your secret is safe with me."

The mention of secrets made me think of something. "Can I ask you a favor?" I hoped he didn't mind.

"Anything."

"You're the first person here I've told about Daisy. I'm not really ready for everyone to know yet. Do you think you could keep it to yourself for now?"

Another pause.

"Is this more of this freak thing you keep talking about? 'Cause, honestly, I just don't see it."

Sigh. "Yes it's the freak thing. I really want people to know me for me before they start seeing me as the murdered girl's sister who was on TV. I know it's a lot to ask."

His turn to sigh.

"I'll keep your secret, Jasmine, with two conditions."

Umm. "What conditions?" I asked warily.

"First, I don't ever want to hear you call yourself a freak again, and second, if any other weird stuff happens, you'll tell me immediately." All of a sudden, he sounded serious.

"It really isn't anything to worry about. It comes with the territory. Worse stuff happened back home and it was nothing."

"Your word, Jasmine."

"Okay, okay. I'll tell you if anything else happens." He definitely drove a hard bargain. I was still a little shocked that he wasn't doing the sympathy thing.

"You should go back inside and get some sleep. Can I call you tomorrow?"

I smiled. "Of course." Had anyone ever said no when he asked that question?

"I'll talk to you then. Good night, Jasmine."

I hung up and sat there staring at the sky for a few minutes. What just happened? I couldn't believe it was that easy. I had been so worried about telling anybody here about Daisy—Easton, in particular—that I couldn't believe it had gone so well.

My next thought brought reality crashing down— something I had completely forgotten about. How was I going to tell my mom that I went on a date?

Chapter 6

When screams rent the air very early Sunday morning, I smiled as I rolled over in bed. Ah, the sweet sounds of revenge. I knew Caedan would be running into my room soon, but not that soon. I was pretty sure he would have to clean himself up first. Simple is the key when planning a prank. Too complicated, and something will go wrong.

It had been easy, really. Thankfully, Caedan had his own bathroom. Some plastic wrap around the bowl in addition to the fact that I *knew* he never lifted the seat, and I was golden—or really, he was. I had made sure we were stocked up with Caedan's favorite non-caffeinated soda on Saturday. Of course, he drank too many before bed, and that was the ticket! It was great being the older, smarter, and patient sister. I never forget. Mean? I don't think so. No one likes a rat. He needed to be taught a lesson.

"You Slytherin! That was disgusting!" Caedan shouted as he ran into my room some time later with his arms waving. Besides pranks, Caedan and I had a mutual love of the Harry Potter books. Not the movies, although both *Deathly Hallows* were pretty good. He jumped up and down on my bed. By this time I was laughing. My mother walked by my room, shaking her head.

"I should have put the video camera in there so I could have seen your face but… eww! Just eww!" I was holding my sides.

"You stink, Jas. That was below the belt. I mean, even for you." He glared at me.

I smiled in triumph. "Don't mess with the master. You know you'll never win."

He bounced right near my head. "Right, that's why you had to come home from school that time because I put sneezing powder in your makeup. And then that time you were embarrassed in class because I put the fart machine in your backpack. I totally got you!"

"And you were suitably punished each time! Don't forget." I smirked at him. He really was a worthy opponent. He was no slouch when it came to pranking, but I didn't want him to get a big head. I was pretty sure I was going to have to be careful for a while.

After church, we spent the rest of the day catching up on homework and getting ready for Monday. While we were all doing the dinner dishes, I was starting to contemplate what I was going to tell my mom about Easton. Did I have to tell her? What if she found out on her own? Would that be a mistake? I didn't want her to start off with the wrong mind-set about him.

The argument I was having with myself was interrupted by the phone ringing. All four of us stopped what we were doing and stared at the phone.

Caedan and I jumped for it at the same time, and he beat me to it. "Buddy the Elf. What's your favorite color?"

Really? Little brothers were obnoxious.

"Oh yeah, she's here. Hang on. Mom, it's for you."

I glared at Caedan behind my mother's back. Insufferable little creep.

My mother answered after the briefest hesitation. "Hello?"

The pause, as she stood there listening, was so long, I just stared.

"I see. Yes, that would be fine. Tomorrow evening will be fine. Thank you for calling. Good night." She hung up the phone and went back to the dishes.

"Who was that?" I asked.

"Oh that?" She wasn't looking at me. She was all of a sudden very focused on the dishes like they held the answers to all life's questions.

"Yes, that!"

"That was a friend of yours. Easton Ward? He wants to drop by tomorrow at five to speak to me."

I stood there frozen while Caedan jumped around the kitchen hooting, hollering, and making kissing noises.

"What?" My voice wasn't working. It came out in a whisper.

What did she mean, "Easton was coming over"? Why would he call *her*? What did he want to speak to her about? How did he get our house number? I was starting to hear buzzing in my ear, and I heard it from what seemed like far away.

"Jasmine! Sit Down. Now!" My mother pulled out a chair and shoved me in it. "What is the matter with you? Caedan stop shouting! Good Grief! Put your head between your legs, sweetie. Breathe. That's better." I could feel the tunnel receding. I wasn't going to faint.

I looked up at my mother, "What did he want?"

"Are you all right now?" She ignored my question.

"Yes, Mom, I'm fine. What did he want? Why did he ask for you? Why is he coming over?"

She sighed. "Well, he asked if he could speak to me in person. He said that you and he had become friends, and he would like to introduce himself. He wanted to know if he could come by tomorrow. I told him he could."

That was all? Why would he do that? Holy Cow, was I in trouble? Was she going to freak out? I sat in the chair staring into space, while Lily and my mom finished the dishes. Caedan was sulking due to my mother insisting on radio silence until the dishes were done and put away. Lily was surprisingly unfazed, and my mother looked lost in thought.

It was time to come clean about the whole thing. Honestly, there wasn't much she didn't know. She hadn't forbidden me to go anywhere with him. I had been in view of friends nearly the entire time after the game. It was time to find out what I was and wasn't going to be allowed to do. If she said I couldn't go out with him, then what? Burn that bridge when I get to it, I guess.

Interestingly enough, I almost felt relieved. I don't like keeping things from my mom. Well, some things. Really, I just don't want her to worry. She'd started acting so much more normal since we'd moved, and I didn't want to change that. I know she's terrified that something will happen to me or the twins. Especially since the Monster was never caught. I just wonder how long we were going to have to live under the you-can't-do-anything-even-remotely-normal-because-something-bad-might-happen rule that has been in effect since Daisy's death.

Will I ever be allowed to date normally or run outside like I used to, because she was murdered? Will Caedan and Lily ever be able to go out with friends or date either? These are all issues we hadn't had to address until now because we were living in a fog until the move. I understand the fear. Trust me. I live with it every day. I have trouble in the dark. I have panic attacks. I am not the same person I was, either, but we moved here to start a new life. I hope she actually lets us.

"Jasmine, let's go up to my room. You two stay down here and finish your homework or read. No TV. Caedan, if I hear as much as a creak on the staircase, I will take your iPod for a week." She gave him the laser glare. "Got me?"

He rolled his eyes while his head was turned away, but said, "Yes, Mother."

My mom narrowed her eyes. "If you roll your eyes up in your head again, I will snatch you baldheaded."

Caedan whipped his head around and stared at my mom. "What does that mean?"

She patted him on the head as she walked by. "It means that Southern women know what's up!"

The picture in my head of Caedan snatched baldheaded distracted me for a moment while I walked up the stairs, but when we got to my mom's room the worry was back.

"I would like to know what's going on with you and this boy." My mom looked serious as she sat on her bed.

"Nothing's going on. He gave me a ride home from school that day, and we've been talking on the phone." My mother looked at me without blinking. I knew that look. It was her I-will-know-if-you-are-lying-to-me stare.

"Anything else you would like to tell me before he comes here?"

I looked down and then back up. This was it. All in.

"After the pep rally, he asked me to go to the diner with him after the game. But everyone went. I just got a ride with him. He brought me back to Julia's house. The girls were at the diner the whole time. I told him who I am." I looked at her. She stared back for a moment, and I could see her processing all the information I just gave her.

"Let me get this straight. You went out with a boy I've never met, without asking me, and without letting me know where you were going to be. We have never discussed the dating rules of this house, and you basically went out on your first date without any discussion. You lied to me, and you expect me to think it is totally fine. Have I got it straight?" I looked back at her for a moment.

"Well, technically, it wasn't a date. The only time we were alone was on the very short drive to the diner and the drive to Julia's house. Absolutely everyone who was at the game was at the diner. I met his aunt, his cousin, and his cousin's girlfriend. We had a sundae, and he gave me a ride back to Julia's. That's it. It was less than an hour, and I wasn't in the car with him any longer than on the day he brought me home.

"I didn't tell you because he asked me after the pep rally, and I just said yes without thinking. I didn't think it was that big of a deal until I was already there. I couldn't have reached him to change the plans anyway because he was at the game. He's very nice and incredibly polite. I'm sorry I didn't tell you. If it had happened differently, I would have told you before I went."

Sometimes I can tell what my mom is going to say before she says it. This was not one of those times.

"Jasmine, I understand you were in a weird position at the moment. Since we have not discussed any particular rules in this area, I guess I can't get angry about the date. I can, however, be upset that you did not tell me after it happened. Did we, or did we not, discuss that you were going to tell me about your life?" She had me there.

"I know, but after it happened I was so worried about you being mad, I didn't know how to tell you. I was trying to decide what to do and then he called! It's like he's psychic or something."

My mom smiled. "All right. I can understand your dilemma. I'm not happy about how you went about it, but I guess I can't prevent boys from asking you out. You haven't told me what he said when you told him who you are."

I was glad she was being rational. "He just said that he was glad to know me and that he was impressed with how I handled myself back then on TV. He said he wouldn't have been able to do it. I asked him not to tell anyone and he said he wouldn't." No need to fill her in on the flowers /running-him-down-the-hallway incident. I would never be able to leave the house again.

"Well, he sounds mature. Do you want to go out with him again?"

Yeah, duh. "Umm, yes?" Did this mean I was going to be allowed? *Please, please, please let her say yes.*

"It's a lot more complicated here to make these kinds of decisions. Back home I knew which kids I liked and which I didn't. I don't even know his family or anything about his background."

At this point, she was pretty much talking to herself. I had learned not to interrupt these little conversations she had with herself. The outcome tended to work in my favor if I just said as little as possible.

"Well, we'll see what he has to say for himself. I am going to tell you right now—if I get any kind of weird vibe from this kid, you will not be going anywhere with him. Am I making myself clear?"

Now it was my turn to roll my eyes. "Yes, Mom. You're clear."

She narrowed her eyes at me. She was probably visualizing snatching me baldheaded.

"If I allow this, there will be rules. If you do not follow these rules, it will be over. Do you understand?"

I was trying to control the big grin that was so ready to be all over my face. I threw myself at her, and we flew back on the bed.

"Yes, yes, yes! I will follow every rule! You're the best mom in the whole world!" My mom just laughed and hugged me back. For one shining moment, all was right with my world.

The next day, I was so preoccupied with my mom meeting Easton that I couldn't concentrate. I had lunch with the girls and took a calculus test. School dragged on, and I couldn't pay attention to anything for very long. Who cared about school? What if she hated him on sight? Or she thought he was weird? Good grief, this could go bad on so many levels.

I was working myself into a frenzy. By the time I got home, I was sick to my stomach. I had seen him in the hallway during one of my passing periods today. I had really wanted to ask him why he had called my mom. Was this some weird Southern tradition? He had been across and down the hall a ways. While I was making up my mind whether or not to approach and ask him, I saw Lisa lurking and staring. I decided I would just have to wait until tonight. I had enough drama to be getting on with.

My mom, Caedan, and Lily were all home when I got there. Mom was cleaning the tile floor in the kitchen when I walked in.

"Hey," I mumbled.

"Hi, sweetheart. How was your day?"

I didn't want her to know how nervous I was about her meeting Easton, but I was pretty sure she already knew. "Long and boring. What did you do today?"

She looked up from the mop. "Cleaned, mostly. Ran some errands."

I nodded. "I'm going to go change."

She was back to concentrating on the mop. "Okay, sweetie."

I ran upstairs, opened my closet, and sighed. I had no idea what to wear. Before, if I couldn't find anything cute in my closet, I would go look in Daisy's. We didn't keep her clothes, of course, because that would just be too weird. It seemed like whenever life would start to appear normal, all of a sudden something would happen to bring Daisy's murder back into the front of my mind. It didn't seem like the pain got any better. I could forget for brief moments, and then the pain was back, as bad as before. Was my life ever going to go back to normal? I had a feeling the answer to that was a resounding no.

So, what to wear when you are down to your own pathetic closet? It was too late to ask Julia, Raquel, or Mandy to come over for a consultation. I am sure they would help, but there wasn't even enough time to do that kind of girl event. Maybe I could call though? Julia was the most laid back of the three. I could see her helping me make a rational decision with the least amount of drama. I called before I freaked out any more.

She helped me go over what my options were and didn't add to my agitation, which was good. We decided on my cutest jean shorts and a flowing white top with my silver sandals. We decided I definitely needed to paint my toenails, and she stayed on the phone with me while I did that, so I didn't have time to get too nervous. I chose a bright pink, and we discussed jewelry choices. I put on my silver bangles and rings and I was good to go. Besides the butterflies that had taken up residence in my belly, I was ready. At four thirty, my mother called me downstairs.

"Jas, I need a couple of things at the store for dinner, and the twins need some stuff at the office supply store for projects they have due this week. Will you run out and get them for me?" She was wiping down the counter and didn't look up.

"Umm… Mom, I…" I fumbled around for an argument. I didn't want to leave her alone with Easton, but I could tell she had arranged it so I would not be present for the "interview." I guess Caedan and I came by our sneaky ways naturally.

"I made a list of the groceries. Oh, and take Caedan with you. He knows what they need." She smiled at me. Great. She wasn't even going to risk leaving me backup. Lily was not good at covert operations. She couldn't be trusted not to cave in under pressure. She was the people pleaser of the family. Well, I guess I could give her the "third degree" later.

I yelled for Caedan and grabbed the list. We took off for the store, and after grilling him about what they really needed, I realized I could probably get everything in one place: Wal-Mart. I was not a huge fan of the store, especially in light of my embarrassing moment in the parking lot. But in this case, getting everything all at one place was a great idea. I was trying to rush Caedan through the store, and once he realized we were hurrying to get home to see if we could catch Mom grilling Easton, he was on board.

Lily's new friend—the one who had broken her phone—had gotten in trouble and had to pay for a new one, so Caedan was giving Lily instructions by text on how to listen in on the conversation.

"I don't know why she is so bad at sneaking around. It's embarrassing!" he grumbled, when he got her latest text.

"Well, it really isn't her thing. Like being nice isn't your thing." I smirked at him.

He grinned back at me. "That's true."

"She says he just got there, and he and mom are sitting out on the porch talking. I told her to listen at the window, but she's scared she'll get caught." He rolled his eyes.

"Tell her she can wear my All Saints bracelet for a week if she listens in," I offered in desperation as we raced around the store trying to get everything in the cart without looking like criminals.

"She says she'll try. I don't know how we are related. If she wasn't my twin, I'd disown her." He had such a disgusted look on his face, I had to laugh.

"Well, mom could have made all three of us go, so I guess it's better than nothing." I had such a cramp in the pit of my stomach. What was she saying to Easton?

"Lily says he's saying that he's sorry for not calling sooner and he should have introduced himself before he took you to the diner." His eyes narrowed at me. "He took you out already? And you don't even know him? What's the matter with you, Jas? Is this guy some creep? Is that why you didn't tell Mom?"

I was shocked. Caedan never expressed concern about anything. Huh. "No, he's not. I already spoke to Mom about it. He asked me to the diner after the pep rally, and I didn't have time to ask Mom. He's really great, Caedan. You'll like him."

He looked away for a minute. "Well, if he turns out to be a freako, I'm gonna go all Jackie Chan on his ass."

I tried really hard not to laugh. I mean, I know he means well. I imagine he feels kind of powerless being the only boy in the family and being so young. It was such a cute side of him. I had a hard time holding back my smile, but I knew he would hate it if he saw.

"All right." I said back. "I'll let you, if that happens." He nodded once, I rubbed his shoulder, and we pushed on.

"Now she says he told Mom how much he likes you"—insert Caedan's gagging noises here—"and that he wants to take you out, but only if it's okay with Mom. Ewww, what a sap! Why's he being such a wuss? That's just wrong!"

All my warm and fuzzy Caedan feelings vanished. That didn't take long, but little brothers were like that.

"He's Southern. It's what they do. He opens my door for me and stuff. You could take lessons. Girls like that." I glared at him.

"Why would I care what girls like? They're weird, and they want to hug you and stuff. Yuck. Anyway, now she says Mom is asking him about his family, and he just handed her a folder. That's weird. What would be in the folder?" Caedan asked, but we were both stumped.

We finally had everything we needed. Mom had a lot on her list. We headed to the checkout. Once we were done, we moved fast. Caedan pushed and rode the cart at unsafe speeds in the parking lot, while I ran beside it. I threw all the stuff into the trunk. We jumped in and were on our way.

Now, I normally obey all traffic laws, but this particular incident required some speed. I pushed the limit a little. When we got off the highway, we hadn't heard anything more from Lily. I slowed down in case they were still out front, and I also did not want to run over any little kids. Pushing it a little on the highway was one thing. Residential district, not okay.

We pulled up to the house, and Easton and my mom were on the porch smiling and laughing like they had known each other for years. What? Who is this guy? What was I getting myself into? Rose Rourke was not easily impressed. She was a good-looking lady. My dad used to say, "Your mother could stop traffic." I have seen many men try to win her over: doctors, patients, salesmen. No deal. She was polite, but I had never seen her swayed in the slightest. Easton must have some serious game. Caedan and I looked at each other sideways.

"What's up with that?" Caedan mumbled.

"Got me," I mumbled back as we got out of the car.

Easton was already making his way to the car by the time I got out.

"Good evening, Jasmine. How was your trip to the store?" He grinned at me as if he knew exactly what was going on. What they say is true. Just because Southern folks talk slow, doesn't mean they're stupid.

"Uhhh, good," I stammered and made my way to the trunk to get the bags.

"I don't think you'll be doin' that now. Let me take those for you." He smiled at me again as he jostled me out of the way and picked up all my bags in one hand. Swoon.

Caedan stood by the passenger door with his mouth literally hanging open. I guess Easton impressed most people upon first meeting. As we walked by Caedan, I reached up and closed his mouth for him.

Easton stopped and held out his hand that didn't have all the bags hanging on it. "You must be Caedan. Nice to meet you. Must be tough being the only guy in the family and so outnumbered."

Caedan shook his hand. "You have no idea," he replied.

Easton chuckled. "Oh, you'd be surprised. If I have to get in a car with my momma and her three sisters…" He shuddered. "Good thing for me it only happens once in a while."

That was it. He had made a friend for life. Caedan had an ally. What was next? Could he win Lily over? She didn't like strange men. I guess we would see.

We walked up to the porch, and my mom was still there waiting for us.

"Jasmine, I've asked Easton to join us for dinner."

I was dumbfounded. What?

"Will you ask Lily to set another place? I believe you will find her right inside." She smiled at me.

I felt like I had walked into an alternate universe. What was going on?

We walked into the house, through the hall, and into the kitchen. Lily was standing by the counter. She looked terrified. Easton set the bags down on the counter. He smiled at Lily and she frowned.

"Lily, this is my friend Easton. He's staying for dinner." I widened my eyes at her, hoping she would pull it together.

"Hi." She was still frowning. Easton was pretty big, and Lily wasn't used to being around big men.

"Hello, Miss Lily. It is nice to meet you." Easton stood back and didn't try to get close. "Do you go to Myrtle Place Elementary?"

Lily's eyes widened. "Yes." She looked officially freaked out.

"I went there too. What grade are you in? Sixth?" Lily just nodded. "Do you have Mrs. Mitchell?" She nodded again. "She's the coolest. Do you know Abby Hardwick?" he asked.

"You know Abby?" Lily looked skeptical.

Easton smiled that swoon-worthy smile of his. "Well, yeah, since she's my cousin. She's one of my favorite people."

Lily gaped at him. "She's, like, my best friend at school. You're really her cousin?"

He nodded. "Yup. And I'm gonna go out on a limb here and say I'm *her* favorite. The competition is pretty fierce. We have a lot of cousins, but I take her and her friends out for ice cream, so—"

Lily was staring. "You're *that* cousin? I'm gonna go text her!" She was grinning as she ran out of the room.

"How did you do that?" I was stumped. "I mean, *really*? My family is not a bunch of pushovers, and you just came in like a wrecking ball and took them all down." He shrugged and started helping me put the groceries away.

"And what's in that folder?" I narrowed my eyes at him. He chuckled.

"Well, uh, yeah, that." He looked a little sheepish. "I kinda wanted to prove that I'm not a psycho, so I put some stuff together for your mom."

I stared at him. "What kind of stuff?"

He was rubbing the back of his neck and looking at the floor. "Oh, you know... resume, official transcripts, SAT scores, driving record, and a couple of recommendation letters. The usual." He looked up at me through his fringe again.

"Are you joking? Recommendation letters? From who?"

He looked even more uncomfortable. "Um... my youth pastor and my football coach."

What do you say to that?

"I figure if I want to spend any time with you, Jasmine, I better be on your family's good side. Besides, they have reason for their concern. I get that. I don't want to be a part of that worry." He looked serious. I was speechless.

I continued to put everything away, when Lily came running in waving her new phone.

"Abby says you should take us out to ice cream tonight!"

Easton laughed. "Tell Miss Abigail that I would be happy to do that on another night." He reached into his pocket. "That would be her now." He smirked and pressed Accept on his phone. "Abigail Jane, how are you this fine day?" There was a pause and he was smiling. "Now darlin', you know your momma will not let you out on a school night. All right—maybe after Finn's birthday on Sunday. Although, I can't see you needin' any more sweets after that. All right, see you then." He hung up. Lily just stared at him.

"Does that mean you're Finn Sullivan's cousin too?" She looked accusatory.

"Guilty as charged. But don't hold it against me. You can't choose your family." The smirk was back. Lily nodded. I'm sure she had a picture of Caedan in her head right then.

"Finn broke my phone," she told him. I was shocked. The kid that broke her phone was Easton's cousin?

"Well, now... He's a bit of a devil, but once you get to know him, he's okay. Would you like me to take care of him for you, Miss Lily?" He looked serious.

"No, I gave him a talking-to and he apologized. He wrote me a nice note, but can you tell him to stop following me around all the time?"

We both burst out laughing.

"Well, Miss Lily, you can't blame the boy for having exceptional taste, but I will have a chat with him for you." She nodded.

"Lily, please set another place for Easton at the table. He's staying for dinner," I asked. She got the silverware and plates and flounced off to the dining room.

"Wow. Small world."

He nodded. "That happens a lot around here."

Dinner was interesting. I let everyone else guide the conversation. I just wanted to watch Easton interact with my family. I was in awe of his ability to make them so relaxed. I looked around and we seemed so normal. Laughing and joking like nothing bad had ever happened. I felt so grateful that my family had some sense of normalcy again. It was like a weight had lifted. We had let someone new into our home, and it was a good thing. God is good. I was humbled by the beauty of it.

Easton laughed with Caedan and teased Lily, but only about how pretty she was and how he was going to make fun of Finn. He talked to my mom about the hospital and her patients and seemed really interested in what she did. After dinner, Caedan asked Easton if he wanted to play video games with him. They had an epic battle of MX vs. ATV Alive on the Xbox. Caedan won. I watched the entire thing, and even though I couldn't tell or prove it, I am pretty sure Easton let him win.

Yup, I was still looking for the flaw. He made sure to leave early enough for homework to get done. I walked him out to his car.

"Well, you certainly make an impression." I was, of course, understating.

"Your family is great, Jasmine. I'm glad I got to meet them."

I smiled at him. "Well, you definitely brought out their bright side."

He was looking down at his feet again. "I was wondering if you would like to return the favor?"

I looked at him warily. "And how would I do that?"

He smiled for a moment, and then took a breath. Was he nervous? "As you may have heard earlier, we have a family birthday party on Sunday for the infamous Finnegan, and I wanted to know if you would come."

Ummm… Family, wow. I mean, I didn't invite him to meet mine. I probably would have waited or put it off as long as possible, and he wants to introduce me to his? Huh.

"So how big a party is this?" I knew he had a big extended family. Meeting everyone at the same time? Whoa. "I mean, how big is your family, anyway? There seems to be a lot of them around here."

He laughed. "Well, I haven't counted lately, but if everyone showed, maybe only sixty or so." Was he joking?

"Only, huh? Just a small get-together, is it?" Even though it sounded a little intimidating, this was one of the reasons I chose the South. I'm fascinated by big families and how they all interact.

"Yeah, well, it could be worse. Some of my dad's side won't be there. They'll be out of town." The sheepish look again. Interesting. What was he hiding? Was there a chink in the armor?

"So where will they be?"

He looked up to the sky and grimaced. "I hate to even say it. It makes them sound worse than they really are." He huffed out air, and then looked me in the eyes. "They're going to a NASCAR race." He looked down and shook his head.

I laughed, and then I had to cover my mouth because I couldn't stop giggling. He gave me a long, suffering look. "Go ahead—get it all out. I know. We couldn't be more of a stereotype if we tried."

Tears were pouring out of my eyes. "Oh my gosh. I'm sorry. It's just so funny. NASCAR? Really?"

He grinned. "I know, I know. I shouldn't have told you, but they'll have it on the TV on Sunday, I'm sure, so…" He shrugged. He was so adorable. He was even blushing a little—just a couple of red spots on his cheeks.

"Well, it's not like I haven't had some seriously embarrassing moments in front of you, so I'm finding it pretty hard to feel sorry for you."

He smiled that slow smile. Holy Smokes. "You shouldn't be embarrassed. We might not have met if Trenton hadn't scared you at Wal-Mart. Then some other guy would have snapped you up before I got my chance."

I crossed my arms over my chest and gave him the glare usually reserved for Caedan. "Yeah, they're just lining up at my door. I don't think so. Nice try, though, Mr. Charming."

He seemed like he was trying to decide whether to say something or not. "What?" I asked.

"Jasmine, are you completely unaware of how beautiful you are?"

I felt the blush work its way up my neck. "I'm going to have to call your Aunt Bellie, because you have the charm turned all the way up tonight. You don't need to say things like that to me—I'm already impressed." I couldn't look him in the eye. Sheesh. Where did this guy learn this stuff? Did he take classes or something?

He grabbed my hand and turned it palm up. He started drawing in my palm. "Jasmine, I know we haven't known each other long, but trust me when I tell you: if I say something, I mean it. You are beautiful to the point where it is scares me. But besides being gorgeous, you are an amazing human being, and I am so glad that you have let me into your life." He looked at me, and his smile made my heart go funny.

All those things you hear about happened. My heart was beating fast, those stupid butterflies had invited their friends for auditions of *Butterflies Got Talent* in my stomach, and I felt like I couldn't catch my breath. Only, it was the good kind of hyperventilating this time.

"I don't know what to say to that, but I'm glad you're the one who caught me." We looked into each other's eyes for what seemed like forever but was in reality probably about thirty seconds. Was he going to kiss me? Until that moment, I hadn't realized we were leaning toward each other. His eyes flicked toward my house, then he straightened up.

"Well, I better head home, it being a school night and all. Can I call you later?"

Why does he keep asking me that? Like I'm going to say no?

"Umm… Yeah, sure." *I am a smooth conversationalist, I tell you what.*

What did he see in me? Every time I was around him my IQ drops twenty points. He leaned in again and gave me a hug. He was so tall and solid, and he smelled so good. I felt safe and warm for that moment. I could have stood there surrounded by his warmth forever, but it was over much too fast. I watched him get in his car. He gave me a little wave and drove away.

Wow. Did that really happen? I felt like jumping up and down and squealing. I controlled myself and walked back up to the house. I realized we had probably been watched the entire time we were outside. Would he have kissed me if my whole family hadn't been staring out the window? Hmmm. Something to think about when I'm alone.

Contrary to what was probably happening just moments before, Mom and Lily were sitting on the couch with their backs to the window reading, and Caedan was at the desk working on what looked like math.

"Did you all have a nice view from the window?" I asked snarkily. Caedan didn't even look up from his work, but he was smirking.

My mom looked up from their book. "Jasmine, I don't know what you are talking about. Do you have any homework you need to get done?"

I sighed and sat down on the couch. "No, I finished in study hall. So he's a total creep, huh?" Now I was smirking.

My mother looked at me with her eyes narrowed. "There's no need for sass. He's a very polite young man, which is more than I can say for you at the moment."

Lily chose this moment to put her two cents in. "Abby says he's the best. He's her favorite cousin, but not because of the ice cream. She really loves all her cousins, even Finn, but she says Easton is the nicest of her boy cousins and has never teased her or put frogs in her bed or held her upside down like all of the rest of them have." She went back to reading.

My mom looked over at me. "Well, he definitely leaves an impression, doesn't he? And he's got more than his share in the looks and manners department. He seems sweet, Jasmine. I think he likes you a lot. I've never heard of a boy bringing an information packet to meet someone's parent."

"What about the rules?" I asked nervously.

"Ah, that. I went over them with him already." Of course she did. I held my eye roll, just in case Easton didn't like bald girls.

"Your curfew is eleven thirty on the weekends. He may visit here during the week, as long as I am home and he's not keeping you from your homework. If he takes you anywhere in his car, you'll need to clear it with me. Also, when you're out, you'll need to text when you arrive where you're going and when you're on your way home. If you're late for your curfew, you'll be grounded a week for every ten minutes you make me worry, and we will also revisit how much time you can spend with Easton. If your grades dip, weeknight visits will be over. And for any change of plans, while you are already out of the house, you'll need to ask first. Is that clear enough for you?"

I just nodded. It was actually pretty fair. Better than expected. I excused myself to go upstairs and process everything.

When I was lying in bed thinking, I realized life was, for the first time in a long time, really starting to look up. There was a gorgeous boy who liked me, my family was starting to heal, and I hadn't gotten any more flowers or weird calls. That had to mean good things in the future, didn't it?

Chapter 7

The beginning of the week went smoothly. I went to class, had lunch with the girls, and did homework. Some things did change, but for the better, which was unusual in itself. Easton actually found me each day and walked me to a couple of classes. We spoke on the phone every day, but not for very long. We both had pretty heavy course loads this year, and homework was starting to take up a lot of time.

I had decided to try out for cross-country. I really loved to run. I used to run track in junior high and was going to try out in high school until Daisy was taken. Until now, it had been out of the question. No sports that would require us to be in the public eye unless the Monster was caught. I had to run on the treadmill at home, and although I ran every day no matter what, I really loved to run outside. My mother felt very differently about this subject and was not okay with me running outside with or without people around. I had discussed it with her before we moved. She assured me that when we moved that would be something I could do again. Not by myself, mind you, but with a group of people. I didn't even ask about running with Easton since she was being so cool about the rules. I didn't want to jinx it. Besides, I would probably be too self-conscious anyway. So, treadmill at home or outside with a group at school. That was at least something.

Today was tryouts. I was pretty nervous. I showed up at the track and was surprised that there was a pretty big group waiting. The coach gathered us up, and I noticed we would be running on the track while the football players practiced on the field. Fabulous. I saw Easton and Chase throwing the ball to each other, but I looked away quickly. I hadn't told him I was going to try out, in case I didn't make it. I hadn't run track in over two years. It really is totally different than the treadmill. I might not even be able to keep up at all. Maybe he wouldn't notice me.

Right. This was not the time to get distracted. I decided to focus on what the coach was saying. He seemed nice, but you never knew about coaches until the season got going.

We did some stretching and conditioning exercises, and then he told us to run. He would let us know when to quit. So I did. The first twenty minutes sucked. They always do. No matter what. Anyone who tells you differently is lying. But after that, I got into this place in my head and it was freeing. I felt like I could run forever, and everything I worried about went away. It sounds totally weird, but I felt very in sync with my body. More so than at any other time, I felt like I was in control. All the noise in my head just stopped. I know it's the endorphins, but I didn't really care why. It just felt great to be running outside again. I was so completely in the zone, I was surprised when the coach whistled. We were done, and it had been an hour. I had forgotten how lost I could get while I was running.

I stopped to catch my breath for a few and get some water, when I heard my name. I looked up, and Easton was jogging over to me from the football field. How is it that he looked amazing all sweaty? I probably looked completely disgusting. On top of it, I wasn't sure if it would be awkward that I hadn't told him I was trying out.

"Hey, how's practice going?" I asked.

"Good, good. Are you trying out for cross-country?"

I shrugged. "Yeah, but I am not sure I'll make it. I haven't run outside in a long time." I looked down and kind of huffed. "You know, safety and stuff."

His face got serious. "Yeah, I can imagine that would have been a problem. Well, you looked like you were doing great. I'm sure Coach Anderson was impressed."

I wrinkled my nose at him. "I don't think so. We'll see. If I don't get on the team, it's no big deal. I just thought I would try. You know?"

He got this weird look on his face about something. "I'm sure it won't be a problem. You cleaned everyone's clock out there. Did you not notice all the kids you passed?" He shook his head. "Jasmine, they were all wheezing and coughing their way through. You blew by them like they were standing still. You amaze me more every day, Jasmine. I would hug you, but I don't want to offend you with my stench."

I laughed. "I'm pretty sure I'm no better. I'm going to take a shower and head home."

"We're all done here. Do you want a ride home?"

"That would be great. Let me check with my mom so we don't break the rules." I rolled my eyes. He laughed.

"I'll meet you outside the gym door when I'm done. Okay?"

Just then Chase and some of the other boys on the team came by on their way to the gym. "That was awesome, Rourke. You kicked some serious booty out there today." There were a bunch of catcalls and whooping and hollering from the team as they made their way in to the showers.

I was probably seven shades of red now. "Uh, thanks."

Easton tried to cover a laugh with a cough.

I narrowed my eyes at him. "Are you laughing at me?"

He shot both hands in the air like I was holding him up. "I'm just a dumb jock on his way to the showers, ma'am." He smirked, and then turned and jogged off toward the gym.

I was about to head off to the girls' changing room when Coach Anderson called me over. "Hey, Rourke, you got a sec?" He was staring at his clipboard.

"Sure, Coach. What's up?" I wasn't sure if this was a good thing or a bad thing.

"Rourke, you ran track at your last school?"

"Um, no sir. I couldn't. Just in junior high school."

He looked up with his brows raised. "So how did you learn to run like that?"

"I, uh… just… you know, run on a treadmill at home every day. I used to run outside every day, but I couldn't do that the last two years." I had noticed that adults don't always ask a lot of questions, so sometimes just a little information was enough.

"Well, you did really well today. I'm really excited to have you on the team."

I must have looked like a fish with my mouth hanging open, but I was shocked.

"Um… so I made the team?"

He grinned and patted me on the shoulder. "Yes, Jasmine. You made the team."

I was in a daze as I walked to the changing rooms. I was shocked I'd gotten on that easily. I was still wondering why he put me on the team when I headed into the showers. A lot of the girls had opted not to shower at school and just changed and left, but I was not getting in the car with Easton smelling as bad as I did. I quickly texted my mom to make sure the ride thing was all right with her.

When I got to the showers, they were completely empty. Now, that was a good thing and a bad thing. Not that I wanted to shower in front of a bunch of girls I didn't know, *but* it started to get kind of creepy when it was so dark, quiet, and empty too. I've seen my share of scary movies, and my own real-life situation was enough to make me a little jumpy. I hurried through as fast as I possibly could and still not stink. While I was by my locker getting dressed, it started to get even creepier because I was completely alone. And there were all these creaky sounds.

All of a sudden, a loud screeching noise came from the shower area. Official freak-out. I didn't care that I didn't have my shoes on—I made a run for it. I hit the door hard and it flew open. Why did this feel familiar?

"Whoa, whoa, Jasmine, slow down. You're running like your hair's on fire. What's goin' on?" I came to a stop, turned around, and of course Easton was waiting outside the door for me looking gorgeous. Just in time to see my mini freak-out.

"I, uh… sorry. I just didn't want to keep you waiting." I looked down. Crap. I can't bald-face lie to him. That's just wrong. When I looked at him, I knew he knew.

"And the noises in the empty locker room totally freaked me out." I put my head in my hands. "I'm so tired of being such a wuss." I felt tears start to choke my throat. I swallowed and forced them back. Then I felt arms go around me, and the amazing smell of him was everywhere.

"Jasmine."

I pushed my face into his chest and took a deep breath. I put my arms around his waist. Can I just stay here forever? This is my happy place. This was much better than running. We just stood there, breathing.

"Are you all right?" he asked softly. He pulled his head back and tried to look down at my face.

I kept my head down and nodded. "Yes. I just needed a minute. Thanks."

I tried to pull away. He held on. "Now don't go runnin' off. I was enjoyin' myself. You are the sweetest thing, and I kinda like it right where I'm at."

I realized how happy he made me, but I felt bad he had to deal with all my ridiculous drama. "I'm sorry I am such a—"

"*Jasmine*—" he warned.

"I just don't think it's fair that you have to deal with all my craziness." I huffed.

He rubbed his chin on the top of my head. "Well, since I'm the one making the choice, I don't imagine you have too much say. Besides, you need to wait to make any judgments about who has the better end of this deal until after you meet my family on Sunday."

I snorted.

"Did you just snort on me?"

I giggled and tried to hold it in. "Sorry."

He rubbed my back and asked, "Did your momma say you could ride home with me?"

I realized I hadn't checked my phone. "I need to see if she texted me back." I reached into my bag. "Yup, she said it's fine as long as we are going straight home. Is that okay?"

He rubbed my back and then stepped away. "Of course. Keepin' your momma happy is very high on my to-do list."

#

On Friday night, I went to the game with the girls, then went to the diner with Easton after. It was a little less nerve-wracking this time. He took me home, and the whole family was up waiting. Big Surprise. No kiss yet, but that was okay with me. I wasn't sure I wouldn't totally panic or do something completely embarrassing. My track record in this area spoke for itself.

When Sunday rolled around we went to church, had lunch, and I then spent an inordinate amount of time trying to figure out what to wear to the "Infamous Finnegan's" birthday party. I called Whitney this time. I knew she would be at the party today, since Chase was Finn's older brother. We had made some inroads to friendship this week, sort of bonding over the football-player thing at the diner. Since we had exchanged phone numbers, I felt comfortable calling. I picked her brain about the dress code at these things.

I was actually excited that I would know a few people there. I really liked Aunt Bellie. I just hoped she hadn't put two and two together yet. Finn had invited Lily to the party as his one non-family friend. Of course, the only reason Lily agreed to go was because Abby would be there. Lily was, however, nowhere near as nervous as I was.

Easton arrived exactly on time to pick us up, and we set off for his aunt and uncle's house. The house was in a more rural area, a ways out of town. There were homes separated by acres of what looked to be small family produce farms. I saw the river peeking through the trees along the road. There was such a different beauty here than in California. There was water on both sides of the road and big trees with branches that swept to the ground. It made for a different atmosphere than we were used to. It was so exotic and Old World–like. Easton explained that most properties had been in the families for many years. They farmed soybeans and wheat, and there were dairy farms out this way too. This farm had been in their family for generations. It was fascinating hearing about his family and how they all connected.

We pulled up to the party, and it looked like the circus had come to town. There were kids of every age, everywhere. There were canopies of different colors all over the yard. Balloons were tied to anything that wasn't mobile and some things that were. An old dog sat on the porch, looking resigned to the balloons tied to his collar. There were kids on horses in a paddock next to the driveway and kids playing horseshoes in a pit behind the house. There was a popcorn machine, a cotton candy machine, and a slushy maker—each with a line about five kids deep, by the patio in back. To add to the circus atmosphere, there was a clown sitting on the grass making balloon animals and surrounded by children. Adults were coming in and out of the house with food for the many picnic tables, mingling on the patio, watching the madness. Toddlers were being led from place to place by older kids.

Lily and I must have looked stunned. I looked over, and Easton had those adorable red spots high on his cheeks again.

"Umm, I know it looks a little crazy, but it isn't always like this… well, kind of—just without the clown. Aunt Bellie really likes birthdays, so…" He looked at me worriedly. "She tends to do it up big."

"Are all these people related to you?" I asked, astonished.

"I know it seems overwhelming, but it won't be as bad as you think. Some are related to my uncles, but mostly, umm… yeah."

Lily piped up. "This is so awesome! There's Abby. See ya." And she jumped out of the car.

He looked at me with concern. "Are you ready?"

I took a deep breath. "Yeah. Let's go."

As soon as we opened the car doors, I could hear circus music playing. I looked at Easton and he grinned.

"She has this thing about atmosphere including all your senses. She's kinda crazy that way."

Crazy or not, I really did feel like I was at the circus. The sights, smells, and sounds were all there. By the time we were almost to the patio, there were children hanging off one or another part of Easton. He had one on one leg, one hanging off an arm, and one on his back. A sweet little girl of no more than three came toddling up, and he grabbed her and shoved her into my arms. "Here, hold this." He smiled at me. She was a pretty little thing with dark hair and brown eyes. She grabbed my face with both hands and smushed.

"Pretty," she said.

"Yes, you are." I smiled at her.

"Well, little Miss Cassandra has impeccable taste," Easton commented as we made our way with our load into the house—to find his parents, I assumed.

The Sullivan's farmhouse was adorable. It was just what you would expect it to look like. Rustic and charming with the homey touches that said a family lived there. The kitchen was a hotbed of activity. Aunt Bellie and two other women who looked remarkably like her were standing between the stove and the refrigerator speaking quickly in a language that sounded French, but not exactly what I learned in French class. The accent here in Louisiana was totally different. They were working together with a synchronicity of movement that spoke of a long history of these kinds of events. Aunt Bellie turned as we came in. She squealed and came rushing over.

"Easton, get those heathens out of here before someone gets scalded! Goodness knows there are enough bodies in here without those little monsters getting underfoot!" Aunt Bellie scolded as we moved into the kitchen from the patio.

"Aunt Bellie, they threatened my life if they didn't get food."

She scooched by us, grabbing the princess I was holding and kissing Easton and me both on the cheek, while herding the little ones out as she went.

"Food will be out in no time. Go get a balloon animal!" She shoved them out the door. "For heaven's sake, you would think they hadn't eaten in a week!" She bustled around the kitchen, grabbing utensils.

Easton introduced me to the other two ladies. "Aunt Sunny, Aunt Cee, this is Jasmine. Jasmine, these are my other favorite aunts." All three resembled each other. They all had brown hair, brown eyes, and were very pretty in an all-American way. Trenton had obviously taken after this side of the family. I smiled at them both, and they shook my hand. We spoke about my time here in Louisiana and how I liked it so far. They were moving around the kitchen quickly, uncovering and filling trays to be taken outside while we spoke. I was amazed at the amount of food they were producing. It must have been quite an undertaking, making that much food, but you would never know by watching them. They made it look so easy!

Speak of the Devil and he will appear. Trenton came bounding into the kitchen from the hallway.

"When are we going to eat, Aunt Bellie? I am dyyyyinnnggg!" He proceeded to drape himself over her.

"Trenton, get off your aunt. You are going to throw her back out, as big as you are now." Another woman had come through the back door. Her coloring was just like Trenton's. Brown hair, brown eyes, and she was very beautiful, even more so than her sisters. This had to be Easton's mother. Right behind her was very obviously Easton's father. Tall; broad-shouldered; dark, almost black, hair—and I was betting the same almost-violet eyes. Genetics were amazing.

"Trenton, you are not dying. Help your aunts carry the food out to the tables." He was grinning. Trenton looked appalled.

"Why doesn't he have to carry anything out?" Trenton whined. He stomped over to me, jostled Easton out of the way, and threw his arm around my shoulders. "He stole my girl, and he doesn't even feel bad! He should at least carry out my share."

I was officially blushing to the roots of my hair. I wanted to pinch Trenton.

"Trenton, you are making Jasmine uncomfortable. Let the poor girl be." Easton's mother scolded him as she made her way over to where we were standing. She opened her arms and gave me a hug.

"It's lovely to finally meet you, Jasmine. I'm Alexandra Ward. You've turned both my boys' heads, and I can see why. You're lovely."

I was speechless. The appeal was not only on one side of this family. Their dad was right behind her. He pulled me away from his wife and gave me a bear hug.

"You're prettier than these hooligans said. Is my son treating you right? If he isn't, you just let me know and I will tan his hide."

I was in a bit of shock. They were so friendly. After the kind of third degree I'm sure my mother put Easton through, I was feeling a bit guilty. I didn't have to prove anything to this family. They were so welcoming.

"It is lovely to meet you, Mr. and Mrs. Ward," I said, after Mr. Ward let me go.

"Please, it's Reese and Alexandra. We are just so happy that Easton is finally dating. I was starting to think that he didn't like girls." Mr. Ward grinned.

"Yeah, Dad, I have been meaning to talk to you both about that," Easton deadpanned. "I was just waiting for the perfect girl. Most parents would be thrilled that I'm picky."

Now I didn't think I would ever recover from my blush.

They asked me how I liked living in Lafayette and if the transition was difficult. We talked about my family and how they liked it here. I didn't know much about them, so it was interesting to hear what they did for a living. His dad owned a classic car restoration shop, which explained Easton's beautiful car, and his mom was an artist. Some of her work was in a gallery downtown. They were very polite, and I felt less nervous than I thought I would.

"Easton, why don't you take Jasmine outside and show her the rest of the farm. It is so lovely in the fall," Easton's mother encouraged.

"I was just thinking that Jasmine has probably had enough of the inquisition, so that's perfect, Mom." He leaned over and pecked his mom on the cheek. He pulled me away from Trenton and led me outside. I could hear Trenton complaining to his parents behind us.

"You see! He just stole her, and he doesn't even feel bad!"

I heard their dad chuckle and say as the door closed behind us, "Son, I'm sorry to tell you this, but you never had a chance."

I looked at Easton. He was smirking as he grabbed my hand. "I love that kid, and he may have seen you first, but I

93

caught you." He turned and looked into my eyes. "And I don't think I'm lettin' go."

My breath hitched. This beautiful, perfect boy couldn't possibly like me this much. I was stunned and scared at the feelings I was having for him. Was this what it was like to fall in love? It wasn't entirely pleasant. I was nervous, embarrassed, and worried. I thought it would feel good and happy—and it did, but it was much more complicated than that.

He was all I could think about. He was amazing, charming, and so good to me. Besides the fact that he was gorgeous, he was just an amazing person who had an amazing family. They obviously loved him and thought he was as fabulous as I did. The little kids followed him around as if he were the Pied Piper, and I could tell that the adults were all so proud of him.

As we walked out to the backyard, his other family members—aunts, uncles, and cousins—stopped him to ask about school and football, and for an introduction. His uncles and male cousins gave him a hard time about me being there, but he was polite and patient with them all. I felt totally out of my league. It was a lot to process.

The food was served, and we all stood around the picnic tables and held hands while Chase and Finn's father, Chad, said grace. We sat at a table with Chase and Whitney. I kept an eye on Lily. She seemed to be doing well with all the strangers. I think having all the kids around made her more comfortable. Finnegan was sitting with her and another little girl, who must have been Abby. The girls were doing their best to ignore Finn, while he was obviously going out of his way to get their attention. Easton introduced me to a few of his other cousins sitting at the table. Apparently his cousin Lucy was Whitney's best friend, and I recognized his cousin Graysen from the pack of football players at the diner. I can't imagine what it would have been like growing up with that much family.

When we were done eating, Easton said to Chase and Whitney, "I'm going to show Jasmine the rest of the farm. We'll see you all later." I was surprised we weren't going to hang out with them, but when I looked up, Chase and Easton did a complicated handshake. There seemed to be some silent communication going on that I'd missed.

We walked past where all the kids were now playing some carnival-type games on the side lawn, and it all seemed so perfect.

"It must have been so much fun growing up with all this family," I mentioned as we were crossing a field away from the main house.

"I guess it was. I don't really know any differently. I love my family, but it has its downside. None of us ever got away with much with as many people watching as we had. Privacy was somewhat nonexistent." He smiled ruefully. "If we do anything wrong, the whole family knows within hours. Bad grades, a scuffle in the locker room, or if I ever went a hair over the speed limit, someone knew about it and told my parents."

I laughed. "I can see how that might cramp your style a little."

He nodded. "It's part of why I haven't dated until now. You see how they are. I'm glad we're here and not at my house. My mom would have brought out the baby pictures."

I smiled. "I would love that!"

He grimaced. Those pink spots on his cheekbones were showing again. "Why did I say anything?"

We laughed a little, trading my-parent-is-more-embarrassing-than-yours stories.

"Is that really why you haven't dated until now?" I was dying to know.

"Well, pretty much. I just hadn't met anyone who was worth going through all that... until now."

"Well, I'm pretty sure your friend Lisa has other ideas. I'm a little worried about turning my back around her. She's a bit scary." I grinned.

He pulled a face. "Yeah, uh, sorry about that. She's a little intense." Those spots got darker. "And you wonder why I hadn't dated until you arrived?"

He had a point.

We came to a pond at the end of the field. There was a small dock, and we walked out to the end and sat down. It was a beautiful secluded spot with weeping willow trees surrounding it. You wouldn't even know it was there if you weren't looking.

"Jasmine, I brought you out here for a reason." He looked out at the water. "I'm not really sure of the right way to ask you this."

Uh oh.

"When I first saw you—"

I sighed. "You mean when I fainted like an idiot?"

"Jasmine, hush. Let me do this." He glared at me to be sure I wasn't going to interrupt him again. I grinned at him and nodded. He smirked and continued.

"When I was holding you in my arms, you opened your eyes and I thought, 'This is it.' Of course, you ran away, and I didn't want to look like a complete stalker, so I didn't follow you around Wal-Mart like I wanted to. It's a good thing too. Your momma would have had me arrested." He nudged me with his elbow.

"Then when Trenton came home the next day raving that he found you at school and how he thought he had a chance with you, I…" He looked down and smiled. "I'd never been jealous of my brother in my life, until *that* day. I grilled him about what you said, what classes you had, everything he knew. Then I told him that you were it for me, and I was going after you. As you heard earlier, that didn't go over so well. We didn't speak for a few days. We finally found a way to resolve it, and then you ran me down in the hallway. I knew I was right. You were even more fascinating than I thought. I couldn't stop thinking about you. I dreamed about you at night. I worried—before I knew what was going on—that something was really wrong, and I wanted to help. I've never felt about a girl the way I feel about you, Jasmine." He looked at me.

I think my brain stopped functioning around the time he said he had been jealous of Trenton. He had to be joking. I couldn't even process everything he had said. How did they resolve it? I was fascinating? He obviously didn't know me well enough. I was the most boring person on the planet. Before I could take it all in, he continued.

"I'm falling for you, Jasmine. I want to be with you all the time. I want you to be my girlfriend." He blew out a breath.

I must have looked shocked.

"Are you okay with that?" he asked.

I nodded.

His smile was slow and beautiful. He started to lean toward me, and right before his lips brushed mine, he whispered, "You can breathe now, Jasmine."

I breathed out slowly, and his lips touched mine—just a brush, and then more pressure. It felt nice. Soft. He turned his head and opened up a little. I couldn't believe he was kissing me and I hadn't made a complete idiot of myself yet. I returned the pressure and relaxed.

After a few moments, he pulled back and smiled. "I've wanted to do that for the longest time."

He grabbed my hand and rubbed my fingers with his thumb. I realized that it didn't matter if I was scared or worried or embarrassed. I really loved this boy and wanted to keep him.

"You haven't said much." He looked concerned. "Are you okay?"

I looked at him. I couldn't be a coward. He had risked telling me how he felt. Now it was my turn. "I'm just so shocked that someone as amazing as you even wastes their time with someone like me. I don't know how I'm fascinating. I—"

He scowled at me. "Jasmine, are you trying to ruin a perfectly romantic moment?"

I knew he hated when I spoke of myself in this way, but truth is truth. "I know that you don't want to hear it, but it's how I feel. I don't say much because it feels like I am going to wake up any moment and none of this will have been real. I'll open my eyes and be in the parking lot at Wal-Mart with a big goose egg on my head. I'm afraid if I say too much, you'll realize I'm not who you think I am and it'll be over."

I looked at him. He was quiet and looking out over the water again. I realized I still hadn't told him how I felt about him. "Easton, I care very much about you. I love spending time with you, and I'm excited and thrilled to be your girlfriend."

He put his arm around me and pushed my head on his shoulder. We just sat quietly looking out over the water. The sun was setting, and for just a moment my world and everything in it seemed perfectly in place. I was glad I couldn't see what was coming.

Chapter 8

Monday morning was hectic as usual, but I didn't care. Easton had asked if he could drive me to school from now on, which led to dropping Caedan and Lily off at their school also. I would have been fine with them still taking the bus, but he offered. Of course, Lily thought that was a grand idea. She especially loved the part in which she would be dropped off at school in Easton's classic Mustang every day. That got worked out on the way home from Finn's party. I had no say. So for part of the drive, it was completely chaotic with Lily and Caedan chattering and fighting in the backseat and Trenton's nonstop chatter. One-on-one time with Easton was not easy to come by.

When we got out of the car in the school parking lot, people were staring intently. I just assumed it was the I-can't-believe-Easton-Ward-is-dating-her bit that I had tried to prepare for. I had caught Lisa glaring at me at the diner Friday night. I had ignored it at the time, but I knew she might become a problem. I wondered how many other girls were going to hate me for dating the most gorgeous boy at school.

The staring continued on as we got into the school. I thought it was a bit strange. Most people had either seen or heard about us being together for the last two weeks. He had walked me to class a few times last week, and we had been at the diner together twice. So why now? I knew our status had changed, but I didn't think anyone else knew. I knew he hadn't changed his relationship status on Facebook. I had checked this morning, Facebook stalker that I am.

Easton held my hand as we walked to my locker. I saw that there was some kind of colorful flyer taped to a bunch of the lockers. As we got to mine, I noticed one had been put on it. I reached up to pull it off and realized it was a newspaper article. There was a picture of me standing behind a bank of microphones with a headline above that read:

MURDERED GIRL'S SISTER STANDS UP TO SERIAL KILLER!
14-year-old calls her sister's killer a coward on the 5 o'clock news.

I knew that story. It ran in the *LA Times* the day after I spoke at that press conference. I just stared at the paper in my hand. On the bottom of the flyer was written in red: "Who Is This Girl?" All of sudden I couldn't think. I could feel the panic start to creep in. Who would do this? Was it the same person with the flowers? Did they think this was funny? My heart was beating fast. Then I felt a hand on my back.

"Give it to me, Jasmine." Easton turned my face to his. "Are you okay?" He looked furious.

"I… umm…" I felt all the blood leave my head. I was starting to breathe fast. "I think I need to, umm…" I could feel my arms starting to shake, and I wanted to run. I couldn't get my brain to work fast enough to figure out what to do.

"Okay, we're going to the office. Come on." Easton grabbed my hand and basically pulled me out of the building and around the corner to the administration office. I could feel everyone staring. Crap. I should have told the girls. My mom was right. They were all going to be mad and hate me. Not to mention, think I am pathetic. My mind was racing. I could feel myself hyperventilating.

"Jasmine, breathe slower. I mean it. It's going to be fine." Easton pulled me into the office. He stepped around the line that had already formed and spoke to the secretary.

"Mrs. Connelly, Jasmine needs to see Principal Thatcher right away." The secretary looked perturbed about being interrupted.

"Mr. Ward, you need to get in line just like everyone else, honestly."

"No disrespect, Mrs. Connelly, but I think it is really important." He shoved the paper under her nose. "This was on her locker and is posted all over the school. Trust me. She *needs* to see the principal." She scanned the flyer and looked up at me, shocked.

"Yes, Mr. Ward, I do believe you're right. Follow me." She pressed the unlock button for the gate leading behind the office counter, and we pushed right through. We followed her through the maze of desks. She told us to wait outside while she went inside the principal's office. I was trying to fight off the panic so I didn't look like a complete moron, but all I could think was "Is he here? Who would do that? How did they find out?" Good grief, Caedan and Lily! I frantically dug around in my bag. The fear, all of sudden, felt very real. What if it was him? What if he was after us again?

"What are you doing? It's okay," Easton said.

"The t-twins… I have t-to check…" I stuttered while I tried to reach my phone.

"Okay. Breathe, Jasmine. The principal will call their school and check. Sugar, you have to calm down."

Mrs. Connelly came back out. "Go ahead in." She patted my shoulder when I passed her. Easton started speaking before we sat down.

"Jasmine is concerned for her brother and sister. They go to Myrtle Place Elementary. Can you please call and check?" As we sat down in the chairs in front of his desk, Principal Thatcher picked up his phone and asked Mrs. Connelly to call and check on Caedan and Lily.

When he put down the phone, he asked, "Miss Rourke, can you tell me what is going on here? Is this you?" He pointed to the picture. Easton was holding my hand and rubbing my fingers with his thumb.

"Yes sir. Daisy was my sister." I was trying to stay calm. Both my knees were shaking, and I kept looking out into the office to see if Mrs. Connelly had found anything out.

"Do people here at school know who you are?" he asked.

"No sir, just Easton." I was starting to feel like getting up and running out of there. I swear I could run to the elementary school faster than they were calling. Didn't they understand that he might have gotten to Lily or Caedan or my mom? I needed to call my mom.

"Sir, may I please call my mom to make sure she's okay?" I needed answers, not more questions. The phone on his desk finally rang.

"Yes? Okay. Uh-huh. I see. Thank you." He replaced the receiver. "Your brother and sister are fine." I exhaled and felt light-headed. "Your mother is on her way."

Wait. What?

"Oh, she doesn't need to come here. I'm fine. I just wanted to be sure she was okay. There's no need for her to come here."

Crap. I was so busy thinking about whether they were okay or not, I wasn't thinking long term. Whoever did this could have just messed me up but good. My mom would not give up until they found out what was going on, and I would never be let out of the house again. Double crap.

"Well, she feels she does, and I have to agree," the principal said.

Oh boy, this was getting out of hand quickly. "Principal Thatcher, I'm sure it was just a prank."

Easton frowned, and the principal was giving me a strange look. "Well, Miss Rourke, that is probably true, but we need to be sure." My turn to frown.

"Do you know who might have done this?" he asked.

I thought for a minute. Lisa's face flashed into my mind. Accusing her was not going to help my situation, however. I didn't know for sure, and I was not a snitch. "Well, it happened only two years ago, and it was all over the news. Someone could have recognized me, or Googled my name, I guess."

He was nodding. "It certainly is easy to get information these days. Am I right in remembering the killer was never caught?"

I looked at him. "That's right. No suspects. Not a clue or sign of any kind. At least none that they told us about anyway."

He looked down at the picture and then right at me. "You were pretty brave to go in front of all those cameras."

I sighed. See, this is the problem. People don't realize it really wasn't bravery. I was furious. At the time, all I could think about was that I wanted justice. We needed to catch the Monster. I realize that will probably never happen. If they haven't found him by now, they probably never will. I did all that for nothing. Bared my soul to the world, and now people think they have a right to my feelings. Guess what? They don't. I just wanted to blend here. Now it's all ruined. Moving was pointless. It will go right back to the way it was. People feeling sorry for me and thinking they know how I feel. Not okay.

"Well, sir, it may seem like it, but really it wasn't. I just thought it was the right thing at the time. It didn't do any good except make it harder to blend in."

Easton had been silent up until this point. He looked right at the principal and asked, "Sir, shouldn't we call the police?"

My head turned toward Easton so fast I felt dizzy. "No! We don't need to do that." I looked at Principal Thatcher "There's no reason to do that. I'm sure somebody just thought it would be funny or was trying to get attention. Don't call. Please." I was starting to feel panicky again.

"Jasmine, we don't know who did this. It is not something to mess with. Your safety is important," Easton argued.

"I have to agree, Miss Rourke." Principal Thatcher was nodding his head. "We can't be too careful. Even if it is just a prank, we don't want to encourage that kind of thing here at school."

All of a sudden, everything felt very out of control. I felt like I needed to reel it back in. I was usually so good at balancing everything, and now it was all toppling over like dominoes. The police? No way. When that show starts, it never lets up. All that would do is bring more attention that I don't want. I don't want to answer endless questions that solve nothing. I know they tried really hard to help, but all they did was turn my life upside down. I couldn't do that again. Not happening.

I fought down the panic. I knew what I had to do. Time for some damage control. I took a deep breath. Here we go...

"I'm sure my mother will agree that it is not necessary to involve the authorities. This should be handled here at school. If a serial killer were here, he would not announce himself by putting flyers up on the school lockers. You and your staff will be much more efficient at finding out who is responsible than the police, who have no connection.

"I know I seemed really worried when I came in here. Now that I've had time to process, it probably is just someone looking for attention or trying to stir something up. Obviously, someone figured out who I am and decided to cause an issue. I would have preferred it didn't come out this way, but there's nothing we can do about it now. I'm sorry I wasted your time." I stood up. "Would it be all right if I waited for my mother in the foyer?"

Sometimes if you act like you are in charge, people will just go along. I was betting on it.

Easton was looking at me like my head had just rolled off my shoulders. Principal Thatcher looked contemplative. I kept my face relaxed and didn't flinch. He drummed his fingers on his desk a few times, then leaned back in his chair. "All right, Miss Rourke, if that is what you want, I will allow it. You may wait for your mother out front. If she would like to speak to me about it further, I'd be happy to meet with her. The custodian has already been told to remove all the flyers, and the staff and faculty have all been made aware of the situation. When we find out who's behind this, I'll handle the situation myself. If anything even remotely like this happens again, I want you to come to me right away. Are we clear?" He gave me a parental-type laser stare.

"Yes sir, and I appreciate your time." I started to walk out of his office, when I realized Easton wasn't following. I turned to face him. "Are you coming?" He was still staring at me. If I wasn't still trying to get away with the con of a lifetime, I would have laughed at the look on his face. Caedan would have appreciated this moment.

"Yeah, okay." He got up and followed me out.

I thanked Mrs. Connelly for her help and made my way out to the hallway. I walked quickly to get to the front of the school, so I could head my mom off at the pass.

"Jasmine, wait." Easton rushed to catch up. I looked at him but kept walking. "What the hell was that?" he barked. I felt the urge to start laughing. It wasn't that it was so funny; I could just feel myself starting to come down from the scare. I needed to hold it together until I was done dealing with my mom. I was still a little hysterical, and if I started laughing now, I probably wouldn't stop.

"What was what?" I widened my eyes at him.

"That routine you pulled in there with Principal Thatcher. I didn't even recognize you. You, like, transformed into Professor McGonagall or something. What are you doing? We need to call the police. I can't believe he let you get away with that!" He was really upset. He wasn't laughing. He looked really mad.

"I know you're worried, but I'm telling you, it's fine. This kind of thing happened at home, and they were just pranks. You have no idea the things people will do thinking they're funny. It would be a waste of time and resources to call the police. They won't be able to do anything. I'm going to talk to my mom, and she'll agree with me. I'm really okay." I smiled at him like there was nothing wrong. He stared at me for what seemed like forever. I didn't blink, but it was tough. I held that smile, then I laughed and told him, "I'm okay." I even rubbed his arm like I was comforting him.

"Jasmine, you are really scary. I just watched you BS your way out of the principal calling the police and walk out of there like nothing happened. If I hadn't seen you minutes before, I would have totally believed this line you're trying to hand me. I'm so angry at you right now that I don't think I can be polite." He looked toward the street and scowled. "Your mother is coming up the front walk, and I'm sure you need everything you've got to handle her just like you handled Principal Thatcher. I'll just leave you to it." He started to walk past me.

He turned back and said, "I was kind of hoping this *was* home, but I guess *that* isn't what I thought it was either." And he walked away.

Oh no. Was this it? Was he done with me? I could feel tears pressing behind my eyes. I took a deep breath and swallowed them back. No time to melt down now. I needed to hold it together and deal with my mom first. So I let him go. I turned and opened the door that led outside.

My mom was almost at the door when I got there. I closed the door behind me and stood in front of it.

"Hey, Mom, where's the fire?" My mom was moving fast and looking determined. Not good.

"Jasmine, are you all right? What happened? Why are you out here? I need to see the principal." I smiled at her and held my hands up.

"I know you're upset, but it's fine. I guess some kids found out who I am. They found that article in the *LA Times* with my picture and put it up on some lockers. It's really okay. Principal Thatcher is handling it."

She looked skeptical. "What do you mean, handling it?" she snapped.

I looked annoyed, hoping this would be believable. "They're taking them down; they alerted all staff and faculty. They're looking into who could have done it. They aren't sure yet, but Principal Thatcher is taking care of it personally. We spoke about calling the police but decided it wasn't necessary because it's probably just a prank. I told him I thought you would agree. I mean, Mom, we know what a nightmare that could be. I really don't want to go through all that again for a prank. Before, there was a reason. I don't want to start that freak show again because someone posted something on my locker. This is why we moved, right?" I had definitely skewed the truth a bit here, but it was important to defuse this before it went any further.

My mom looked thoughtful. Another laser glare. "You're right. Locker posting is probably a kid's prank. I know you don't want this kind of attention here. It's enough that everyone will know now. Are you okay?"

Hmmm… How to answer that one? I didn't want to slip too far to the dark side here.

"I was a little scared at first when I saw it. I was shocked, I guess. Easton was with me, so after I heard that

107

everyone was okay, I realized it was just a prank. Not looking forward to dealing with all the people I didn't tell. I know you want to say 'I told you so' right now." I smirked at her. Off topic is better.

"Jasmine, I wouldn't do that." She looked concerned. "I just want you to be happy here. I'm sorry you have to go through this. If they're your real friends, they'll understand."

I nodded. "I know, Mom. I'm sorry you came all the way over here. I'm really fine."

She looked me in the eye again. "No fainting or panic attack?"

Thin ice here. "No fainting. A small amount of panic when I first saw the flyer. Easton helped." The mom I knew from before Daisy's murder was showing herself more and more. It was getting tougher to get anything by her.

But she seemed placated. "Good. I'm going to go talk to the office and let them know they are to call me about even the smallest thing, Jas, okay? This is no joke. I'm glad you handled it, but we aren't taking any chances here, you got me?"

Boy, I don't think I had gotten three laser stares in one day, ever, but at least we were on the downhill side. "Okay, Mom. I know. I love you." She gave me a hug, and we walked into the building.

I waited while she spoke to Mrs. Connelly. Then, I got my note for being late and headed to class. I was not looking forward to the rest of my day, but at least I had gotten over the immediate hurdles. The next two were just as daunting: the girls and Easton.

How would I explain this? All of a sudden I was exhausted.

Chapter 9

Walking into class late was not exactly helping my situation. I had AP US History with Mrs. Lowe, and of course, when I walked in and gave her my note, everyone stared. I sat down next to Julia as quickly as possible and proceeded to fix my gaze at the front of the class.

After the rumbling settled down and the lecture continued, Julia passed me a note. Here we go. If Julia was mad, the others would be furious. I held my breath and looked down.

Are you okay?

Whew. She didn't sound mad. I chanced a look at her. She looked concerned, not angry.

I wrote back: *Yes, just a little freaked out and worried, now that everyone knows. Is everyone mad at me for not telling?*

I passed it back and waited with my knees bouncing up and down. She wrote back quickly. *Not mad, just worried about you. Who would have done that? Put it all over the school like that?*

Okay that's good. Not mad. At least I'll have a chance to explain at lunch what is going on. I wrote: *Idk. I really would like a chance to explain myself to you guys. Do you think we could meet somewhere quiet at lunch?*

Julia looked like she was thinking. She shoved the paper back over when she had finally written her answer. *How about on the bleachers at the football field? There's usually no one there at lunch.*

What a relief. I nodded at her. I had drawn enough attention today, so I tried to focus on the last bit of class. I hoped my friends would understand why I hadn't told them about Daisy. I really wanted to make a new start here. It had been going so well. I couldn't even think about Easton right now. Those compartments were filling up again quickly, but they were there for a reason. Some of them needed to stay locked down tight.

At lunch, I headed over to the bleachers right from class. I couldn't eat even if I wanted to. My stomach was in knots. I hadn't seen Easton since he walked away this morning, and for reasons I could only guess, that particular compartment wouldn't stay locked down. I felt like all my nerves were on the outside of my skin.

I stopped at the bottom of the stairs to the bleachers and prayed. I prayed that my friends would understand why I hadn't told them about Daisy and my former life. I also asked for the right words to tell them my story.

This is it. No more procrastinating. I made my way up to the bleachers and looked to see if anyone was already there. Mandy and Raquel were sitting at the top, and I saw Julia making her way from the other side. I sat down in front of them, one bleacher down.

"Hey." I smiled at them. They both started talking at once.

"What's going on?" Mandy looked concerned

"Are you really that girl in the picture?" Raquel looked irritated.

"You guys, give her a second to catch her breath!" God bless Julia. "Go ahead, Jas. You have the floor." She glared the other two into silence.

"Thanks so much for meeting me and taking your lunch to do this. I am going to tell you whatever you want to know, but there are two things I want to ask of you. The first one is this: please don't be upset that I didn't tell you before. All the attention is a problem for me. I hate it, and it's part of why we moved. I didn't tell anyone here, except Easton, and I really didn't have a choice, which I will explain shortly. Second, please, *please*, do not feel sorry for me or my family. We're fine. I absolutely hate people feeling sorry for me. It happened. It's over and we moved here to move on with our lives." At this point they were all nodding. Good so far.

"Now, having said that, here goes. I'm that girl in the picture. Daisy was my older sister. She was kidnapped and murdered by whom they assume is a serial killer. They have never caught him and they probably won't, unless he does it again and messes up, because apparently he covered his tracks well, and they have no clue who he is. I only told Easton because he saw me in a situation that led him to ask a bunch of questions I couldn't answer honestly without telling him who I was. Trust me—I tried to get away with it, and he didn't let me. So, I know you have questions. Fire away." I blew my breath out hard and waited.

They all had stunned looks on their faces. I knew they couldn't decide what to ask first. "What situation did he see you in?" Mandy asked.

"You know that story I told you about running him down in the hallway?" They nodded. "I sort of lied to you all. I am so sorry, but I just wasn't ready to tell you this part of my life yet. On top of that, it was more embarrassing than I originally told you. Since Daisy's murder I have had a bit of a problem with panic attacks. Do you guys know what that is?" They nodded again. Should I be worried they weren't really speaking?

"Certain things set it off. Dark parking lots and hallways are not my friends. When I came out of class that day, it was dark in the hall where my locker was because of the storm, so I was already feeling a little creeped out. Someone put flowers in my locker or bag—I'm not sure which. Daisies and jasmine wrapped in yellow ribbon. I opened my locker and they fell out. All I could think to do was run. So I did, and I ran Easton down." I looked at them sheepishly. Julia and Mandy kind of chuckled, but looked horrified at the same time.

"Who would do that? Put that in your locker? Is it the guy? You know… him?" Mandy said in an almost whisper.

I shook my head. "No, no. People do all kinds of weird things when they hear about these kinds of stories. Back home, in California, people did weird pranks like that too. But the thing is, there, I was ready for it, you know?" I could tell it was a lot for them to take in.

"So why did Easton ask all those questions?" Julia wanted to know.

"Well, the fact that I acted like a crazy person when I landed on him and was hyperventilating and crying might have clued him in." It was almost funny now—or it would be if he wasn't furious with me after my "performance" in the principal's office.

"Are you kidding? That is embarrassing. I know you said you hate sympathy, but I'm sorry. That is just sad!" Mandy joked.

I laughed. "Oh no, you can feel sorry for me about that. That was awful. So, after he took me to my locker and saw what I lost it about, he knew something was up. He kind of kept after me till I told him." I wrinkled my nose. "I really felt like a fr-… idiot, then."

Up until this point, Raquel had not seemed really engaged in the conversation. She was playing with her phone, and I wasn't even sure she was listening. When she looked up to speak, she appeared irritated. "What did he say when you told him?" Raquel asked.

"He was surprised and remembered me from TV. I wish I had never spoken up in front of the cameras, but he said he was impressed with what I had done and was proud to know me." I shrugged. I looked away from them and mumbled, "I wish that was still the case." They all looked surprised.

"What is going on? Is he upset with you?" Mandy asked.

"Uh, yeah. I'm pretty sure it's over. He's really angry about something I did this morning, and I can't and wouldn't change it so… yeah. That's my story. I'm sorry I didn't tell you sooner, but I really didn't want people looking at me and thinking only about what happened. I wanted you all to know me for me, first. I didn't know when I was going to tell you, but I would have. It was just nice being me without the baggage for a while, ya know?"

Raquel spoke up. "I'm sorry about your sister and all, but I don't like being lied to."

"You're right. I should have told you the whole story and not just half-truths. A lie is a lie. I'm sorry."

"Well, it's not like she didn't have a reason. I can't imagine how awful it must be to lose your sister like that. I get why you wouldn't come out and tell us everything right away." Julia glared at Raquel. "It's not like you don't stretch the truth a bit on a *daily* basis."

Raquel cracked a smile. "True. All right, you're forgiven. I guess it makes sense why you did it."

"Do you really have no idea who put those up?" Mandy asked

"I bet it was Lisa. She's off the deep end." Raquel made a crazy motion with her finger. "And she really hates you now."

"I wouldn't put it past her. She really is a nut when it comes to Easton," Mandy agreed

It almost relieved my mind thinking it might be Lisa. I wasn't totally convinced, but she was a lot less dangerous than the other option. At least I had worked it out with the girls.

"Thanks for listening, you guys. I am glad you aren't mad."

Julia reached over and gave me a hug. Raquel and Mandy threw themselves at us, and we were in one big group hug pile on the bleachers. One more down.

After school, I went to cross-country practice. Thankfully, we weren't running on the track. The coach had given us a set course of five miles. Since we were just getting started, he would check our time when we got back. I was so happy to be running outside. I needed to get out of my own head today, so even the first twenty minutes didn't suck as bad as they normally did. When I made it back, I realized I must have passed everyone else because I was the only one.

Football looked like it was just ending. I didn't know if that was good or bad. I had asked one of the girls before practice if she would give me a ride because I was pretty sure Easton wasn't going to be doing that today, even though I had cleared it with my mom this morning. I skirted the field as best I could and made it back to the locker rooms—without being seen, I hoped. I showered quickly and decided to wait for Shelby out by her car. I didn't want to stay in the empty locker room, and I didn't want to look like I was waiting for Easton, so I figured that was my best choice.

He was standing by a pole right outside the door when I came out of the locker room. His face was grim as he stared at the ground. He looked up when the door opened. I was pretty sure this was it. I felt tears prick the back of my eyes. I blinked and bit my tongue. I was so tired. I didn't know if I had one more emotional confrontation in me today, but I knew I didn't want to cry in front of him. Especially not if it was over. He didn't need my baggage. He shouldn't have to deal with all the crap that was my life. I almost wanted him to walk away, so he wouldn't have to deal with it. It wasn't fair to him. I would just let him go, and he didn't have to feel guilty. If I cried, he would feel bad.

Okay. Suck it up. I jabbed my palms with my fingernails and walked over to where he was standing.

"Hey." I looked him in the eye. He looked tired and hurt. I wished I could do something to fix it, but how could I change it? I would do the same thing if it happened again. I smiled at him. I wanted him to know I was okay with what he was going to do. It was all right to leave me.

"Don't do that, Jasmine. I can't stand it." He looked away.

"Do what?" I guess I wasn't doing a very good job. Why did everybody buy it but him?

"Pretend you're fine when I know you aren't. It's what got us here in the first place."

I didn't know what to say, so I stayed quiet and literally bit my tongue again not to cry.

Out of nowhere, he grabbed me and pulled me into a hug. It shocked me so much that once I breathed him in, I started to sob. This was not the pretty kind of crying, mind you. This was the great big gulping, ugly kind of crying. He put his chin on top of my head and rubbed my back.

"I'm sorry, sugar. I shouldn't have gotten so angry this morning. You scared me so bad I didn't know what to do with it all. You wouldn't let me help you. I was shocked that you could put on that kind of performance. I've never seen anything like that. It upset me that you could do that and fool everyone around you. What if I believed you when I shouldn't? Please tell me you won't do that to me, Jasmine, I don't think I could stand it."

I snuffled a few times and tried to lift my head, but he wouldn't let me, so I just turned it.

"You aren't leaving me?"

He chuckled. "No ma'am, you are not getting rid of me that easy."

I gulped. "I think maybe you should. I'm an awful lot of trouble."

He pulled my chin up. "You're worth it." He smiled.

I got serious. I took a step back out of his arms. "I mean it, Easton. I know you don't like what I did. But I would do it again. I'm not worth all this drama. I'm sorry you had to deal with all of this when you shouldn't have to, but I can't allow things to get out of hand like that. You don't know what that kind of sideshow is like. I don't want you to think that I've changed my mind about calling the police. I don't want to go through that again."

He looked grim again. "I pretty much realized that when you let me walk away without a word, Jasmine." He shook his head. "You are some kind of stubborn, huh?"

I didn't smile this time. "I just know that that kind of attention brings nothing but pain and trouble. It invades your life and it never, ever, stops. It's why we moved. I cannot allow my family to be dragged back down into that when things are starting to go back to normal again."

I wanted him to understand the seriousness of the situation. I would do whatever it took to keep my family from experiencing that again, even if it meant giving up something or even someone I loved.

He was looking at me thoughtfully. "You know, at first I was angry because they believed you. Then I was shocked that you could lie that well."

"I wasn't lying. I—" I started to protest. He held up his hand to stop me.

"Jasmine, you manipulated and twisted that situation to such a degree that the principal went against what he knew to be right because you were that convincing. I don't know what you call that, but where I come from, that's wrong." He looked upset still.

"But when I thought about it more, I realized that you were doing what you thought was right. What I was seeing must have been what we were all seeing on television two years ago. That must be why people didn't recognize you easily. It was an act. I get it now. You use that ability to get through the difficult situations in your life. Especially when you feel out of control like you did today."

He paused for a moment, took a deep breath, and went on. "As much as I understand why you did what you did to me, the principal, and your mother, I don't ever want to see that again. It was disturbing, and you have to promise me if we are going to work this out, you will never do that to me again. I hate being manipulated, and even if you think it's for a good reason, honesty is always better. I want your word, Jasmine—your promise—that you won't ever do that to me again. Even if you feel threatened and feel like you have no other option, I want you to trust me."

How did he know? How had he discerned so quickly what was going on? I didn't even understand myself that well to be able to articulate it like that. I knew that I had this ability when I was scared or mad to become someone else. Hide the real me and put forth a persona that wasn't at all what I was really feeling. Could I promise to never do that to him ever again?

"I think you need to clarify what you mean by 'do that again.' If you mean argue my point of view, I will for sure do that again. I won't allow my family to be dragged through that kind of circus again. I'll always do what I can to stop it. The pretending-to-be-fine-when-I'm-not thing is a little harder to promise, only because I don't really know when I'm doing it. Out-and-out lying—that, I will promise not to do again. I'm really sorry." I looked at him hoping to see forgiveness. He was staring at me with a contemplative look on his face.

"I can agree to that. Are you really all right now?" He looked stern.

"Yes, I'm better now. Much better."

He grabbed me for another hug. "Okay, let me get you home, then."

I texted Shelby on our way to his car, letting her know I didn't need a ride. I was so relieved we had worked it out. I knew I had to try to always be honest with Easton or this just wasn't going to work. I couldn't imagine what it would be like for me if it didn't. I already loved him. I was so relieved that he wasn't going to leave me, I felt dizzy. I couldn't imagine how awful that would have been. I never wanted life to go back to the dull, pathetic way it was before I met him. He was quickly becoming the most important person in my life. As scary as that felt, I was really going to try to do the things he asked, but I knew it would be difficult.

I've never been a big sharer of my feelings. In my family, it was hard enough to have any privacy. Everyone seemed to know everything about everyone. I had to work to keep what I could to myself. Except with Daisy. I told her all my secrets. She was a great secret-keeper. Obviously a little too good. Since her murder, I hadn't found anyone I wanted to share any of my secrets with. Now, maybe Easton could be that person. I had made a considerable effort in keeping all of my difficulties, like my panic attacks, from everyone. It was going to be interesting to try to change that now.

The rest of the week was fairly uneventful, with the exception of all the whispers and staring. Not very many people had the nerve to ask about Daisy, and the ones who did were pretty nice about it. No one was overly sympathetic. I definitely didn't feel the weight of pity. I think that because it hadn't happened in Lafayette and two years had passed it wasn't the same as before. I didn't feel as pathetic. People were more curious than anything. Surprisingly, getting over that hurdle was easier than I could have thought possible. I still felt some coolness coming from Raquel's direction. It was as if she didn't trust me now, but I understood that. I would just have to work hard to earn that trust back.

The football team had their first away game on Friday, and my mom actually let me go. We all loaded onto a school bus. It was a lot of fun, even though I didn't speak to Easton until after the game. Even then, it was brief. We were all waiting by their bus when the team arrived, after winning the game by a landslide. We whooped and hollered appropriately, of course. When Easton saw me, he picked me up and twirled me around. Then he drew me a little ways away from the crowd and put his arms around me. I was in my happy place.

"I wish I could ride home from the game with you, but I have to go with the team. No girls allowed." He grimaced.

"It's okay. I'm with the girls, and we've had a good time. I'll probably just fall asleep anyway."

"Well, that sounds like the bus I want to be on. Not stuck with a bunch of smelly football players."

"I'm sure you'll be fine." I laughed. I did really wish we could ride back together. This week, it had been difficult to find time to spend together with practices and homework.

"Well, I was wondering, will your momma let you go out tomorrow night too? I mean, on a real date. You know—a nice dinner, like a real couple? With me?"

I giggled. "Oh, with you? I don't know. I thought you were talking about some other guy. I don't know if that would work."

He gave me a look. "All right, Miss Smart Mouth, we'll just see. I guess I'll have to call your momma myself. Maybe *she'll* go out with me without any sass." He was grinning.

"Well, since she thinks you're all that, I'm sure it won't be a problem. You don't have to call her. I'll ask when I get home."

A real date with him. Nobody else around. Just the two of us. It sounded perfect. Would my mom let me go? Well, no way to find out until I asked. She really did think Easton was great. It didn't hurt that Lily and Caedan adored him. It was hard not to be impressed with how naturally he had fit into our family.

When he gave me a hug, there were catcalls and whistles coming from the windows of the bus. Then we heard the coach's voice from the door. "Ward, I hate to interrupt your love life here, but seeing as you are a captain,

I thought you might want to be on the bus with the rest of your team when it leaves."

Easton put his forehead on mine. He groaned. "Gotta go." He kissed my cheek and took off at a jog.

"Comin', Coach. I was just kissin' my girl after our big win." He turned and blew me a kiss while he hung out the bus door. My heart was racing. Would I ever get used to his charming hotness? My guess was no.

When I got home, my mom was waiting up. Wasn't she tired? I knew she had worked all day. I never figured out how she functioned on so little sleep all the time. She was, however, looking so much better—even in just the few weeks we had been here. Her skin looked healthier, and she had put on a little weight. She didn't look like a refugee anymore. I couldn't believe how much our lives had changed for the better since arriving in Lafayette. All my worrying turned out to be for nothing. Moving here had been a good choice.

I sat down with my mom on the couch to catch the last of *Letterman*.

"Did you have fun at the game, sweetie?"

"Yeah, it was really good. We won. Easton played really well." If I couldn't brag to my mom, who could I brag to?

"I'm sure he did. Everything that boy does is amazing, right?" She was grinning at me.

"Umm, yeah. Pretty much." It felt weird to talk to my mom about Easton, but I had to tell somebody.

I always hesitated to bring up my dad, but I wanted to know if all these feelings I was having were normal. Is love this uncomfortable? So up and down? I wanted to ask her these questions, but I wasn't sure that she wouldn't get all overprotective.

"Did you feel like that about Dad when you started dating?"

She laughed. "Oh yes. Your father was quite a charmer. Don't you remember? Even the ladies in the grocery store would be practically swooning by the time we left. I was crazy for him. The accent didn't hurt either." She looked almost embarrassed.

"I have never seen you charmed by anyone, Mom. I can't believe that worked on you." I was laughing now. I couldn't imagine my mom feeling about someone the way I did about Easton. Weird.

"Well, believe it. It happens to the best of us. I learned my lesson, though. There needs to be more than a charming personality under all those good looks. Trust me." She sighed.

"Mom, was it really that bad?" I was starting to get annoyed. I know my dad had issues, but he loved us. I also knew it wasn't always enough.

"No, sweetie, it wasn't, and that was part of the problem. Your Easton, however, is the real deal. I don't say that lightly. You know that. He's a great kid. I'm happy he realizes what an amazing girl you are." She reached over and squeezed my hand. Time to go in for the kill while she was feeling warm and fuzzy.

"So, speaking of Easton, he asked if he can take me out to dinner tomorrow night. Just the two of us. Is that okay? We'll be in by curfew." I put on my best puppy-dog face.

She looked thoughtful for a moment. "I'm sure that's fine. Where's he taking you?"

"He texted me the name and address on our way home. I'll forward it to you. Thanks, Mom." I got up from the couch. "I'm goin' to bed. Love you."

I looked at her before turning to go upstairs. She really was beautiful. I was sad she was still alone. Maybe I should start looking for someone nice for her. Hmmm…

When Easton picked me up the next night, I wasn't nervous—just excited to be spending time with him alone. It seemed like whenever we were together, someone else was always there. When we got in the car after the expected interrogation by my mother, we just sat for a second. He turned in his seat to face me. "Hi."

"Hi." I smiled at him.

"I missed you."

"Since yesterday?"

"Yup." He leaned in and kissed me. My heart did funny little jumps in my chest. He pulled away after not long enough and grinned. "Jasmine, you look amazing tonight. I am going to have to chase the other guys off with a stick." He started the car and pulled away from my house.

I hated when he said this stuff to me. It was nice, but it made me feel so uncomfortable. "I know you Southern boys feel it necessary to always be complimenting girls, but you don't have to do that. I know how plain I am. Daisy was the beautiful one. I got the height. It's fine with me. I don't like standing out. Being the jolly blonde giant is enough."

He chuckled. "It shocks me how clueless you are about your own looks. It's one of the things I love about you. Most girls are completely self-absorbed." He shook his head.

"I think you just felt sorry for the new girl. You were probably one of those kids who brought home the ugliest stray dogs and cats and begged to keep them, weren't you?" I poked him in the arm.

"You think I felt sorry for you? Huh. Interesting." He nodded. "So, you know when your cross-country team runs on the track during football practice?"

"Sure. My favorite. I love running in front of you and all your buddies. Good times," I snarked.

"Have you looked up in the bleachers lately, Princess Oblivious?" He was grinning.

"Umm… no. Kinda focused on not falling on my face. Why?"

"You haven't noticed that the large crowd of guys watching keeps getting bigger?"

"You're making that up. And even if it's true, it isn't because of me." I scowled at him. Now I was getting annoyed.

"Right. I'm sure it doesn't have anything to do with the addition of the gorgeous leggy blonde running around the track, looking way too attractive in her running shorts and tank top. Trust me—they aren't there to watch football."

"Okay, you, that's it. Give me your phone. I'm calling your aunt."

"She would back me up on this one. If those guys don't stop drooling every time you run by, I'm gonna have to teach them a lesson in manners." He looked stern.

"You're crazy. You know that?"

"Well, a man's got to protect his own, sugar." I was sure he was exaggerating to make me feel good, but it was cute in a caveman sort of way.

The drive wasn't very long, and we were soon downtown. It was an interesting little area. The streets were blocked off. There were canopies set up with live music and vendors all over. Cajun music could be heard the minute we opened the car doors.

"I know we're eating early, but they have this Art Walk thing once a month down here. I thought we could walk around and look in the art galleries and museums after. The live music is usually really good too."

"That sounds really nice." He had put a lot of thought into the date. No dinner and a movie for Dream Guy. I should have known. "Will we be able to see any of your mom's work?"

"Yeah. I think you'll like it. It's really good. Of course, if I don't say that she'll take a switch to me, so…" He shrugged. Could he be more adorable?

We were apparently going to a Cajun restaurant. When we got there, we were seated right away in a nice, quiet table in the back. Easton pulled my chair out for me. I felt like we really were a couple. Even though it wasn't technically our first date, it felt like it. Thankfully, some of the embarrassing first-date stuff was out of the way.

As we checked out the menu, I decided to let him choose for me. I had no idea what I might like in a Cajun restaurant, so why not? It was one of those things you see in movies that I had always wanted to do. Having the guy order for me sounded so romantic. It also solved the worry of ordering something too expensive. Dating was so complicated.

"Jasmine, what would you like?"

"You can just choose for me. You've been here before, right?"

"My family comes here a lot. We like to each order something different and pass it around.

"That sounds fun. I'm not picky, so you choose."

"All right, but don't hold it against me if you don't like it. Although, I haven't had anything here I didn't like. Where does your family like to go? Have you tried any of the restaurants here yet?"

"No, we really haven't gone anywhere since we moved. My mom's hours are long, so we really don't go out. I remember when my dad was with us, he would take us out all the time. We used to go down to Chinatown to this really authentic Chinese restaurant. It even had ducks hanging in the window. It freaked me out. I never would eat duck when we went."

"You never talk about your dad. Do you mind me asking what happened to him?"

"No, I don't mind. I just don't think about him much anymore. He's been away so long, and so much has happened. He was from Ireland. Did I tell you that?"

"No, I knew you must be Irish with the last name Rourke, but I didn't know your dad was actually from there."

"Well, he immigrated here on a temporary work visa. He met my mom and they fell in love." I pulled a face. It was difficult to picture that my parents ever felt that way, now that I had serious feelings for Easton. Yuck.

"For whatever reason, after they got married, he never got his citizenship. That was when they were really cracking down on people getting married just to get US citizenship. One night, he got into a bar fight. It wasn't completely his fault. Some guy was threatening his girlfriend, so my dad stepped in and beat the guy up pretty bad. My dad is a bit of a hotheaded Irishman. He was arrested and deported.

"My mom was really angry. She told him that if he couldn't put his family first, it was over. She wasn't going to drag us to Ireland when he couldn't be responsible. He had some trouble with drinking, and I think she just figured her life was easier without the drama. He was a good dad when he was around, but not terribly consistent. Then, he was just gone."

"What about after what happened to Daisy? Did he come back?"

"No, he wasn't allowed. Even for the funeral. He was kicked out of the country for ten years. He has three or four years left before he can apply again. He used to call a lot, but after Daisy, we really haven't heard from him. He sent a beautiful letter to be read at her funeral and then… nothing."

He looked thoughtful.

"I told you I come with a lot of drama." I gave him a fake stern look. "You can't say you weren't warned."

"I was just thinking that you've had a lot of sadness and loss in your life."

"Well, lately it's been looking up." I smiled at him. I really was smiling all the time now. My life was going so well, it was kind of scary after the years of bad stuff.

We ate and laughed the rest of the evening. Dinner was amazing. Sharing our food was romantic. We walked around downtown Lafayette, looking at lots of art. Some we liked, some we hated, and some we didn't understand why they called it art. We went to see his mom's, which I loved. She had this mysterious kind of unique style. She painted gorgeous landscapes of the countryside in Lafayette: swamps, rivers, and beautiful sweeping trees. I was incredibly impressed.

Our date had been so amazing, I wished it would never end. As we drove home that night with the windows down, I prayed and prayed that my life would stay exactly the way it was at that moment.

The next night, I was thinking about Easton and how perfect the date had gone. I was surprised at how good my life was going. Maybe God just felt I deserved a break.

Unfortunately, my break officially ended.

As I was getting ready for bed, my phone rang. I flung myself onto my bed to reach my purse on the floor on the other side. By the time I wrangled out my phone, I just answered without looking at who was calling.

"Hello?"

I heard music playing low, and then it got louder. It was the song they'd played at Daisy's candlelight vigils. I was stunned. The only people who would know that were in Los Angeles, not here in Louisiana. I could feel myself starting to hyperventilate. What was going on? I hung up.

Really? Are people this cruel? Do they think that's funny? Who would do something so awful? I hated that song. It's beautiful, but awful. They only used it because it had her name in it. That song did not represent my sister. My sister was full of life and happiness. Not at all like the song talked about. I had a minor temper tantrum when we planned her funeral. I didn't want that played. My mother agreed.

Now I was fuming. Great. I would have to tell Easton, and he was going to freak out, but I had promised. This is where our agreement was going to get difficult. I didn't want to tell anyone about this. As much as I wanted to be honest, I knew this was all related to the stupid flyers last week. I knew Easton wouldn't see it that way, and he would want me to tell my mom or something. Ugh! I needed to calm down first. I would take a shower, think about what I was going to say, and then call. A plan was good.

Now here is the thing with plans. Ever heard the saying "When we plan, God laughs?" Yeah, well, it's totally true. Or I plan and Caedan laughs. And then he is tortured within an inch of his life.

I turned on the shower and got in. It was fine until the water got hot and then... tea. Yup, he had put tea bags in the showerhead, and I was doused with hot tea—peppermint, to be exact. My favorite. "Ahhhhhhhhhh! Caedan! You little creep!" I yelled. Of course, by the time the tea came through, I was washing my hair, so I had to rinse out the shampoo, and now I smelled and was covered in peppermint tea. I jumped out of the shower, grabbed a towel, dried off, and threw my clothes back on. In the mood I was in, he was going to suffer. Big. I stomped down the hallway on a mission.

"Caedan, where are you, you little cretin? Don't think you can hide, either. I *will* find you!" I heard giggling from Lily's room. Aha! He thought she would protect him. I think not.

I flung open the door. "Where is your evil twin? And don't think you can hide him. It won't go well for you." Lily was sitting on her bed pretending to read. She was grinning and finally looked up at me.

"I... uh... don't know." She looked down at her book and then sideways at her closet. Boy, he was losing his touch. I flung open the closet door and saw the toe of his sneaker peeking out from under Lily's laundry pile. I grabbed his feet and pulled.

"You little freak! Did you think you could hide from me? You are done!"

By this time, Caedan was shouting, "Let me go! You weren't supposed to shower until tomorrow morning."

This explained a lot. He was probably thinking he would get out early and catch the first bus, so he wouldn't see me until after school. I had veered off my normal schedule and messed up his plan. I held him down and started tickling him. I know this sounds too nice for retribution, but you have to understand how much Caedan hated to be tickled. It wasn't funny to him. It was torture. Just what was called for.

"Are you trying to make this better or worse for yourself?" I knew I wouldn't be able to pull this off for very much longer because he was getting bigger, but for now it worked.

"Okay, okay, stop, stop. I'm sorry." He was writhing around on the floor trying to get away.

"I don't think so. Sorry for what? Sorry you got caught? Sorry I showered tonight and not tomorrow morning? What are you sorry for?" I was sitting on him now, while I tickled him, and he was miserable.

"Sorry, just sorry."

Hmmm…"Well, what do you need to say to get out of this mess, Caedan?"

"Okay! Okay! Jasmine is the Most Beautiful High Queen of Pranks, and there should be a statue in her honor. Okay, please stop," he gasped out while trying to catch his breath. I laughed and got up off him.

"That's right and don't you forget it." I narrowed my eyes at him as he stood up. I held my fist out to him, and we fist bumped. "Nice one." We smirked at each other. "Watch your back." I threw that remark over my shoulder as I went back to the bathroom to take out the tea bags and shower again.

As amusing as torturing Caedan was, I was still hearing those song lyrics in my head. Those compartments were getting really full again. I really didn't want to tell Easton about that phone call. Why did my life have to be so complicated?

Chapter 10

In all the craziness of the night before, I ended up not talking to Easton and telling him about the music call. It took me longer than I thought getting the showerhead off and then back on. I had to scrub to get the peppermint smell off me. It was too late to call when I got into bed, so I just texted him good night.

The next morning we weren't alone for even a minute. The twins and Trenton were in the car, and they all seemed to be talking a mile a minute. Lily decided to relate the entire tea bag/shower incident to Easton and Trenton. I realized, at that moment, my sister was not entirely without guile. She had them engrossed in the whole story.

First, she related how juvenile she thought Caedan and I were with our many past pranks. She made it sound like she was forced into helping Caedan. She played up the twin connection that, on a normal day, she thought was ridiculous. She made the entire caper sound like a super-secret CIA mission with detail and precision planning. She had them laughing and shocked at points. Then she wrapped the story up in a pretty little bow for them. I could tell they thought she was a riot. I sat quietly, smiling. I didn't chime in because she was pretty fair in the telling, and I was so happy to see her acting like her vivacious self again, I couldn't bring myself to interrupt.

"Jasmine, I can't believe you are such a prankster. That doesn't seem at all like you." Easton was grinning.

From the backseat, Caedan mumbled under his breath, "Shows how much he knows."

I turned and glared at him. When I turned back, I told Easton that I really only pranked when it was necessary to crush evildoers. He smiled. "Yes, ma'am, I can see that."

After we parted ways before first period, I didn't see him the rest of the day. I had PSAT testing and didn't have a regular schedule. Our school was hosting our first cross-country meet this afternoon, so our talk would probably need to wait until tonight. I was a little nervous about the meet, since I hadn't competed in a few years, but overall I was excited. My mom couldn't make it because of work. This was a first, but Easton and Trenton both said they would be there at the end to watch me cross the finish line.

After school, I went to the girls' locker room and got changed for the meet. There would be three other schools there, so it wasn't a huge meet—just a small one to start off the season.

We all lined up and took off at the gun. I told myself to get my head into that space where I could run and not worry about where everyone else was. After about ten minutes, it worked. We had a 5k run to finish, and that seemed easy. The route was beautiful and took us along a twisting road where the trees grew thick by the river. The colors on the trees were starting to turn just a little, and I was enjoying the experience.

I had pulled out in front and was by myself, when I heard someone coming up behind me. I was about to kick up my speed a little to stay ahead, but I was jerked off my feet by my hair. Pain shot through my head and I gasped. What was happening?

I tried to jerk out of their grasp, but whoever it was had a tight hold.

I landed against something hard, and the air whooshed out of my lungs. I was being dragged into the trees. It happened fast. I was spun around and dragged some more. I took a big gulp of air to scream, but before I could, he pressed his hand over my mouth and nose. The real panic hit. I couldn't breathe.

Whoever he was, he was big. I could feel him behind me. His chest was big and he was strong. I was trying to kick and thrash to get away, but I got no leverage. He shoved me up against a tree. The side of my face dug into the bark. He kept himself behind me so I couldn't see him at all. He had my ponytail wrapped up in his hand and was using it to hold my head in place against the tree.

Tears were pouring down my face. I knew I was supposed to be doing more, but I couldn't think. The fear was so big it was choking me.

Just as I was starting to get dizzy from lack of oxygen, he loosened up his hold on my face a little.

"Breathe, Jasmine." His voice was a low whisper. He had his mouth up close to my ear. I could feel his breath on my neck. He pushed his whole body up against the back of mine. "If you scream, I'll have to knock you out sooner. You don't want that, do you?"

I realized then who this was. It was him. I knew it. Terror ripped through me.

How was he here? How had he found us? I felt everything start to go black around the edges. I was going to faint.

He shook me hard.

"Stay with me here, Jasmine. I need you awake for the next few minutes so I can get my point across. Do you understand? Nod if you do."

I nodded.

I was trying to breathe and stay focused, but I was starting to feel nauseated. I needed to think and not panic. I needed to remember everything, figure out how to get loose, get away.

"All right. Good girl. You know who I am, don't you?" I nodded. "Smart girl. I knew you would catch on quickly. Let's get straight to the point then. I have some instructions for you, and you will do them exactly, won't you?"

I nodded again. I was trying hard not to vomit.

"See, I knew it would be easier dealing with you than it was with Daisy. Did you like my little serenade last night? I needed you in the correct frame of mind for today. Are you ready to hear my instructions?"

I nodded even thought it felt like my head was on fire.

"You will get rid of that guy you have been spending so much time with. You will tell him it's over. I don't like to share. I don't want to see you talking to him or his annoying brother ever again. Do you understand me, Jasmine?"

I nodded again. He increased the pressure on my hair. It felt like it was coming out at the roots.

"This is not a joke." His whisper turned harsh. He pushed me harder up against the tree. I felt the bile burning my throat. "If I see you so much as glance his way, I will kill him, his brother, and his favorite cousin, just for the inconvenience you are causing me. You belong to me, Jasmine. I saw you first, so he loses. Get rid of him, or you will have all of their deaths on your conscience. Do you want that?"

I tried to shake my head, but I couldn't. He must have gotten the gist.

"Good, good. You may not go to the police. You may not tell anyone. If I see you or any of your family near the police, I will take Lily and you will never see her again. Are we clear?" I was nodding my head as much as I could without ripping out my hair. "We are almost done here. When I call you the next time, you will answer and you will come to me, won't you?"

Tears were pouring out of my eyes again. Not Lily. I could never let that happen.

"Yes," I whispered against his hand.

"Good girl. You're mine, and I will come for you soon. Be ready." Then all of sudden a piece of material was covering my face. I gagged. Everything went black.

I woke up with my face in the dirt. When I turned over and looked up, the trees were spinning. How long had I been here? Was he still here? I looked around and realized I was alone. This was why he knocked me out—so he could get away without me seeing him or what he looked like. My head was fuzzy. I tried to stand and almost fell over. I started to sob. I couldn't believe what was happening. I was gasping and trying to catch my breath, but it felt impossible to get control. My whole body was shaking, and I couldn't stop it.

What do I do? He's here. All this time, he had seemed like a character in a book or a movie. Not exactly real. More like a fairy tale you tell your children to keep them scared. Well, he was as real as it gets. And scarier than I thought possible. The one thing we had feared the most had come true.

I leaned over and vomited into the dirt. My stomach wouldn't stop heaving. I finally drew a deep breath and wiped my mouth. I felt the shakes and the panic coming again and fought them back. No. I could not give in to that. The Monster was after my family again. He needed to be stopped. And now I knew what I was dealing with.

I had to pull myself together. Make a plan. It was the only way.

I tried to brush myself off, but not much was going to help how I looked. I wobbled toward where I thought the road was. It took me about five minutes to find it, but I got there. I knew I couldn't run. My balance was still way off. I felt woozy and slow. I started back the way I came, thinking that would be shorter, since I hadn't been halfway when he grabbed me.

As I got closer to the school, there seemed to be a lot of people running around and looking freaked out. Oh no. This couldn't be about me. I saw what looked like most of the runners in a bunch standing by the finish line. Apparently, I had been out awhile. So, making up a sprained ankle was not going to work. I needed to think fast, but my head felt like someone had stuffed it full of cotton. I couldn't think straight.

I saw Easton at the top of the stairs in the front of the school. He was pacing back and forth while he was on the phone. I made it to the bottom of the steps. I saw Trenton standing off to the side, looking as white as a sheet. I was about to call out, when Trenton saw me.

"East, she's here. She's here!" He was running down the stairs toward me, when Easton's head whipped around and he saw me. Trenton grabbed me and was shouting, "We've got her! We've got her! She's here."

All of sudden, there was a buzz of voices, and I heard Easton tell whoever was on the other end, "She's here. No, she looks all right. I'll see you in a minute." He hung up, ran down the stairs, and practically ripped me out of Trenton's hands.

"Are you okay? What happened?" He pulled me into a hug and then pushed me out again. He started rubbing his hands up and down my arms. "Are you hurt?" He was looking me up and down. I looked around, and people were starting to gather. People were shouting, but I couldn't really hear what they were saying.

"I… um… I'm fine. What's going on?"

Easton looked confused. "Jasmine, you've been missing. The meet is over, and you didn't come in. Everyone has been looking for you. We didn't know what happened to you." Just then, I heard sirens in the distance. That was all bad. They could not come here. No police. He would know. The shakes were back, and I couldn't stop them this time.

No, no. I just, I… I think I just fainted. I got overheated, so I went to stand in the shade. When I woke up, I got a little lost and couldn't find the road."

"Did you fall? You look scraped up." He was checking my arms and face for injuries. "Did you hit your head?"

"No, I'm okay." I was going to start crying if I didn't pull it together soon. I could not do this now. "I'm sorry." I looked up. The paramedics, fire department, and police were all pulling into the parking lot. In the car directly behind them was my mother.

The paramedics got there first with their gurney and insisted on checking me out. I didn't want to do this. I wanted to go home. Easton stood right next to me while they asked me questions about what happened. As I told them the story, I knew it was thin, but they seemed to buy it. I watched my mother run from her car to where I was sitting with the paramedics. She grabbed me.

"Jasmine, you scared me to death! Are you all right?" I had a huge lump in my throat.

"I'm fine. I got overheated and must have passed out when I got into the shade. I'm so sorry."

She was checking me over and asking questions of the paramedics. "Mom, really, I'm fine. I want to go home. Now." I looked at her. "Please, Mom? We don't have to talk to anyone, do we? I just want to go home." I was begging now. I knew I sounded pathetic, but I needed to get her and myself out of there before the police decided to start asking questions. They were already talking to Coach Anderson. I couldn't risk it.

"Okay, sweetie, drink that water and we'll go." My mom was still dividing her attention between me and the paramedics. She was in full nurse mode, asking them questions about my vital signs and whatever. Easton was practically glued to my side.

"Sugar, are you sure you're all right?" He had this look on his face, like he wasn't sure he believed me. Well, he was pretty smart, wasn't he? He should never believe me. He should never believe me again. Well, he wouldn't have to, would he? It was all for the best. I knew it now. I probably wasn't going to make it. It had been so easy for the Monster to grab me. I had been fooling myself all this time. Thinking the calls, texts, and flowers were nothing. He could easily get to me and anyone I loved. He was a killer, and he wouldn't stop until he got what he wanted. I had to get away from Easton and his family. I had no choice now.

Everything seemed like it was coming at me from the other end of a long tunnel. Like I wasn't even a part of what was happening around me.

"I want to go home." I couldn't look at him, so I looked down at my shoes. They were totally scuffed from when the Monster had dragged me through the trees. Huh. Weird. I didn't even feel scared anymore.

"I'm really tired." I must have laid down on the gurney, because the next thing I knew, I was on my way to the hospital in the ambulance. Honestly, I didn't care. I was so tired, I closed my eyes again.

The next time I opened them, I was in a hospital room with the machines beeping, and it was dark outside. My mom was asleep in the chair, and Easton was standing at the window looking out.

"Hey," I tried to say, but it came out more like a weird frog croak. He turned his head and smiled at me. He came over to the side of the bed and sat down on it.

"Hey, Sleeping Beauty, I've been waiting for you to wake up. I was going to try to kiss you awake, but I thought your momma might object," he whispered. I grinned at him, and then everything came rushing back and it turned into a frown.

"Why am I here? I don't remember exactly. I know I wanted to go home, but I was so tired."

He was still smiling, but his eyes clouded over. "Well, you fell asleep on the gurney, so they decided it would be best to keep you for observation."

I nodded. "Wait, if my mom is here, where are Caedan and Lily?" I started to sit up. They couldn't be left alone. The Monster could change his mind and decide to take Lily, and he could hurt Caedan in the process. "She didn't leave them alone, did she?"

He looked perplexed. "No, no they're fine. Lily's at Abby's house, and Caedan's at Finn's. They're fine. Relax. It's all okay, sugar." He pushed me back down on the bed. "Besides, if you aren't quiet, you will wake your momma, and she just fell asleep a bit ago."

"What time is it?"

He looked at his watch. "Two thirty."

I gaped at him. Where had all that time gone? What had been on that fabric? Was that why I was so tired? I didn't need to be sleepy. I needed to think. I needed to make a plan. I was the only one who could stop the Monster. He needed to be caught. I would do this because I had no other choice. But I knew first that I had to end my relationship with this beautiful boy who owned my heart.

I felt like my chest was being squeezed in a vise. I loved him more than I had even known up to this moment. Now that I knew I would have to give him up, it was so clear to me. He was it for me. This must be what love is. I wanted to curl in on myself and sob my heart out. But I didn't have time for that now.

I didn't know how I was going to do this, but it had to be. I couldn't risk being seen talking to him ever again. The Monster would kill him without hesitation—and sweet Trenton and Whitney's Chase. I didn't have the power or ability to protect them all, and the Monster knew it. I could not even think of the heartache it would cause in so many lives. It was too horrible to contemplate. I, more than anyone, knew the horrendous things this murderer was capable of. Their beautiful family would be destroyed like mine was. And then I would not be able to live with myself.

They could not die because of me. I could prevent it, so I would.

The question was how to make breaking up with him believable? It didn't matter that I was breaking my promise never to lie to him if I was ending things, I guess. I took a deep breath. *Please God, let him believe me*. I know it will be a lie, but is it wrong if it saves his life? God must have been listening because I got the perfect opening.

"Jasmine, you really scared me today. You need to take your personal safety more seriously. I don't know how else to express to you how important you are to me. You scared everyone." He looked serious.

"Easton, we're going to have to talk," I started. "I know I told you I wanted to be your girlfriend and all that the other day, but after today, I think I changed my mind." He looked stunned. I had to ignore him, so I looked at my blankets. "I realized that I'm not ready to be as serious as you are. I don't really want to answer to you—or anybody, for that matter."

I took a breath and poured on the gas. I looked right at him and said, "I mean, having to answer to my mom is enough. You are such a nice guy." Ah, the kiss of death. "I just don't think it's working. I'm really sorry if I led you on."

My mom needed to stay asleep right now. It would be too hard to lie to both of them so blatantly. I had all I could handle with what I had going on.

"What are you talking about, Jasmine?" He looked confused and bordering on pissed off. I put on my stubborn face.

"I told you, I'm just not ready. I've never dated, and I think I committed too soon. I'm too young to be in a committed relationship. You're always asking where I am and what I'm doing. You act like you're my dad. My dad isn't here, and I like it that way. I like you a lot, but I don't think this is working," I repeated. I looked down at the blankets and back up again to see if he was buying it. He was just staring at me, not saying anything. He looked like he was trying to decide something.

"Jasmine, you promised me," he said angrily.

Time for the big finish.

"What? The lying thing? Easton, I'm not lying. I'm so sorry. I don't want to hurt you. That's all. I don't think it's working out, and I don't think I should stay with you because I feel bad. That isn't right." I looked into his eyes that were so beautiful and hurt at the same time. He held my gaze for what seemed like forever. And then he nodded.

"All right, Jasmine. If that's what you want. That's what we'll do." He leaned down, kissed my cheek, turned around, and walked out the door without another word. That was it. Heartbroken in seconds. It was shocking how fast it could happen. From happy to miserable in no time at all.

I scooted down in the bed, pulled the covers over my head, and sobbed myself to sleep as quietly as I could. My mom never even stirred.

The hospital released me the next morning. I was still a little dazed from whatever had been on that piece of material and the breakup with Easton. I really wanted to curl up in a ball in my bed at home, but I insisted on going to school. It didn't seem wise to avoid it. I was worried about what might happen if I wasn't there. The Monster was obviously watching. What would he do? I wanted to prove I was doing what he said. I had gotten the beginnings of a plan in the early morning hours before my mother had woken up, and I needed to get on with it.

When my mom dropped me off midmorning, I thought I was ready to face the questions and the staring. The girls were really sweet. They had baked me cookies and brought them to school. We sat around at our table in the quad munching them at lunchtime, which worked out well since I hadn't brought or even thought about lunch. Into this setting, the ever-grating Trenton arrived. He marched up to me, grabbed my arm, and pulled me out of my seat.

"Trenton, stop it. What are you doing?"

He glared at me. "You're coming with me. You obviously hit your head when you passed out yesterday or I wouldn't have to ask you what the heck you are thinking." His face was in my face, looking very upset.

"What are you talking about, Trenton?" I protested as he dragged me a few feet away from where the girls sat.

"I'm talking about you breaking up with my brother." He was angry.

I understood why he was upset, but this was my chance to make a clean sweep. I was just going to convince them all that they didn't know me very well, and that I was just a vapid, flighty girl who didn't know her own mind. "Trenton, this is none of your business. We broke up, okay? No big deal. He wanted to be more serious than I did. I mean, he was constantly telling me what to do." I was really pouring on the shallow-girl act here, but this was Trenton, and it took a little bit of doing to get through his thick head, I knew. I just needed him to stay angry and stay away from me.

"What are you talking about? One day you're ecstatically happy, and the next, you're just over him? I know it might seem weird to you because I was saying how mad I was, but, Jasmine, he's devastated. How could you do this to him?"

He looked like I just kicked his puppy. "I just don't want to be told what to do by anyone, okay?" I glared at him. "That goes for you too. Just go away, Trenton."

He looked stunned. I could only take so much. I turned and did the best imitation of Lily flouncing away that I could manage. I didn't look back.

The girls tried to look like they weren't watching what happened, but I could tell they saw the entire thing. I sat back down at the table and tried to act nonchalant.

"What in the world was that about?" Mandy asked right away.

"I broke up with Easton last night, and Trenton obviously thinks it's his business." I shrugged for effect. Here we go. Let the onslaught of questions begin.

"What?" Mandy kind of screeched.

"Are you kidding? Why?" Raquel looked like someone slapped her.

"Oh, Jasmine, are you okay?" Julia. Gotta love her. She was always looking out for me.

"Yes, I'm fine. I had a very good reason. He wanted to be too serious, too fast. After my little overheating incident yesterday, he lectured me about my personal safety and how I needed to be more careful, and I got upset. I have a mom. I don't need a dad. I don't want a boyfriend who thinks his job is to tell me what to do. That's all. His idea of a relationship is not the same as mine."

They looked at me like I had lost my mind. Well, if I were them, I would think so too. Give up Easton for that flimsy a reason? I would have to be crazy, but thankfully they didn't know me that well, so I could be. I just needed them to buy it for now. I needed to put some distance between me and everybody I cared about, to keep them safe. The Monster was obviously watching somehow. He knew what was going on in my life. I wouldn't put it past him to threaten my friends too.

"I'm sorry if that's a problem for all of you. I'm going to go to class." I got up from the table and walked away. I knew I had hurt their feelings, but really it was what was best for them. I was dangerous to be friends with, and I needed to focus right now. Keeping to myself would give me more time to plan anyway.

I couldn't believe my life had come to this. Everything had been going so well, I guess I should have known. This must have been what happened to Daisy. When I think back to the time before she was taken, she had been acting a little strange. Distracted and jumpy. He must have threatened her too. It made my stomach cramp to think of how scared Daisy must have been with no one to talk to. It made me sick to think that he used me to get to her. She must have felt so helpless.

But this time it would be different. I was going to change the game now. I knew what he was capable of. All of this destruction of our lives was going to be for a reason. My plan still needed work, but I thought I might have something. I had a lot of research to do. FedEx was going to be my new best friend.

As scary as it sounded, my attitude was "bring it on." I would be ready. I would make sure he got caught. I didn't want to die in the process, and the idea was to come out alive on the other side, but there were no guarantees. The police hadn't caught him before, and I was pretty sure he had covered his tracks here as well, so I couldn't alert the authorities. I couldn't risk my family or Easton's. There was really no other way. This Monster had ruined my family and killed my sister. I wasn't going to let him get away again. I would never be able to live with myself if someone else got hurt.

The next few days I spent a lot of time planning and not allowing myself to think about everything that could go wrong. I made myself scarce at school. I sat as far away from the girls in class as I could. I was being ignored by them overall, but Raquel gave me some pretty hateful looks a few times. I ate lunch by myself and avoided the common areas. Whenever I saw Trenton, he acted as if I didn't exist. Even though it was exactly what I had wanted, it made my week that much worse.

At the end of the week, I finally was allowed to go back to cross-country practice. I knew it would be difficult because today we had to stay on the track. Of course, football was having their practice at the same time. I got out on the track and tried to get out of my head from the beginning, but seeing Easton on the field running drills and passing the ball made the first twenty minutes that much more torturous. I was just hitting the point where my run stopped sucking so much when I rolled my ankle.

"Rourke! You okay?" Coach bellowed across the field, so most heads on the track and the field turned to look at him and then me. Brilliant. Could I do anything that wasn't noticed by the entire population of Lafayette High

School? Of course not. That would be much too simple. I limped around the corner and hopped my way to Coach. Out of the corner of my eye, I saw Easton turn, start toward me, and then stop. Sigh. This was my life now. When I got to Coach Anderson, he sat me down on a nearby bench.

"What happened out there?" he asked as he manipulated my foot in different directions.

"I don't know. I was just coming around the corner and my ankle rolled." I winced a few times.

"All right, Rourke, you're done for the day and probably for a week or two. Ice, ice, ice. Every twenty minutes tonight and then every day after school. Do you have crutches at home?" Of course we had crutches. In fact, the entire closet in the utility room was full of first aid supplies. My mother could probably outfit a small hospital from what she had stored in there. "Yeah, Coach. A few pairs actually."

He chuckled. "Accident prone, are we?"

I smiled. "Not really, but my mom's a nurse, so…"

He smiled back. "Oh, that's right. Well, keep me posted on how you're doing for the next few days and we'll see when you're up to coming back. Okay?" I nodded and started to hobble my way to the gym. All of a sudden, I was scooped up off the ground.

"Wait, what are you—?" I looked up and Easton was carrying me. My brain stopped working. No shock there. "I, uh, you don't have to—"

"Shut up, Jasmine." He was looking straight ahead and kept walking. Ooookay. I shut up and looked where we were going instead.

It felt so amazing to be in his arms. I wanted to bury my face in his chest and breathe in. I didn't care if he was sweaty. I know—gross—but I had missed him so much. I wanted to just stay where I was forever, but what if the Monster had seen? This was very dangerous. We were almost to the gym.

He set me down in front of the girls' locker room doors. "Thanks." I didn't even look at him. I thought I heard him sigh. But I hopped my way through the doors and didn't look back. Oh please, Lord, don't let the Monster have seen. Crap. That did not go as planned at all. Well, I was just going to have to try harder not to be anywhere he was. The sprained ankle had solved the practice problem. It just had to be enough.

By the time I got home, I felt like I had run the gauntlet, but there wasn't any time for rest. I had spent a lot of time doing my research on the computer, and I still had a lot to do. My plan was coming together, and I hoped it was fast enough. Not having to go to practice would help me out quite a bit. Unfortunately, the bane of my existence thought he had dibs on the computer. I didn't think so. I had seniority, and I was in no mood to negotiate.

"Caedan, move. You're done." I gave him a little shove to get him out of the chair. My package had come today, and I really needed to get it set up. I didn't have the patience right now to deal with an obnoxious little brother.

"I don't think so. I was here first." He didn't even look away from the screen. I could see he was playing one of his favorite games on Nickelodeon's website.

"I need to get some work done, you little creep, so move. You can play later." I gave him another little shove. My stuff needed to be done before my mom came home. I was thankful she had been working a lot of shifts this week, otherwise I would need my own laptop, but that wasn't going to happen. Sharing the computer with Caedan could be a problem. Especially right now.

"I was already here, so just push off. You can have it later. Just because you don't want mom to see what you are doing. I'm not moving."

I paused, a little stunned. "What are you talking about? I'm not doing anything but e-mailing people back home," I said. "I also have a history project due. Homework comes before your game, Caedan." I already felt like I was coming out of my skin. The Monster could call me anytime, and I needed to be ready. I felt like the clock was ticking, and I was so far behind. I didn't want to deal with an annoying brother too. Lily and Caedan had been taking the brunt of my worry all week. Thankfully, I think my mom told them to tread lightly due to the breakup with Easton.

He turned in his chair and smirked at me.

"What's all that stuff you've been looking at online then? A project?"

I gritted my teeth and refrained from dumping him out of the chair. I didn't have the time or patience for his antics. "As a matter of fact, it's a project on how far technology has come in the last 150 years and what part the US played in it. What did you think I was doing, dork?" He looked crestfallen. It was like I had ruined his whole night. Ah, well, age and wisdom beats young and clever—at least this time.

"Oh. Well, I just thought you were going to be keeping track of Easton, now that you're the biggest idiot on the planet and broke up with him."

I glared at him. "Why would I do that? I'm the one who broke up with him, genius." Crisis averted. "I'll call you when I'm done. It won't be long. I just have a couple of things to research."

He slunk out of the chair and mumbled, "Jerk." I ignored him. He was a little too smart sometimes. I really needed to remember that.

That night I went to bed early, complaining my ankle was bothering me, and after being subjected to it being shoved in a bucket full of ice water numerous times throughout the evening, it certainly wasn't a lie. Life was *so* not what I wanted it to be right now: angry friends, no boyfriend, ice baths, grumpy brothers, and a crazy serial killer after me. It was time for bed.

I was hobbling back from the bathroom when my phone rang. When I saw it was a blocked number, I was terrified to answer it, but then again—what would happen if I didn't?

I answered the call and heard the voice I dreaded to hear.

"Jasmine." My breath caught and my heartbeat sped up.

"Yes," I gasped out as I hopped quickly into my room, shut the door, and fell down on my bed.

"Didn't we have a conversation about you getting rid of that oaf? He had his hands all over you. My instructions were clear."

I knew he must have seen me with Easton today. Crap.

"Yes, I'm sorry. I took care of it."

"Be sure you stick to our agreement or it won't go well for him. Do you understand?"

I was shivering all over. "Yes, you don't need to hurt anyone." Please let him believe me.

"It won't be long until we're together." *Click*.

I crawled under the covers. I set my alarm and reached into my nightstand drawer for the only picture I had of Easton and me together. I held it to my chest. What if I couldn't save him or my family? I cried myself to sleep. Again.

#

There are rules to getting away with something. You can't leave any detail undone and think it won't matter— that's how you get caught. It's all about the planning. Details are important—ignore them at your peril. But it's important to remember that you'll never think of everything.

My alarm went off at two a.m. When I got up, I put on my darkest running clothes and crept down the stairs as quietly as I could. Stepping over the creaky stair in the middle, I made it downstairs and safely out the back door.

I was ready to go. I had activated the GPS that was strapped to my "bad" ankle. I needed to make sure it worked the way it was supposed to. This was my test run. I started to run down the sidewalk on my way to the trees at the end of the street. I noticed movement in the car in front of me and my heart started to pound, but it wasn't the Monster.

It was Easton's car. What? His driver's door swung open. What in the world was going on?

I started to veer away from the car to the trees, when he got out and called me.

"Jasmine." I came to a halt on the passenger side. He was scowling. "What are you doing?"

Was he kidding? What am I doing? What was he doing? He could ruin everything in this one moment. I looked at him, then glanced at the trees.

"Don't make me manhandle you into the car. I am not in the mood to be patient right now." He looked like he meant it.

I looked at the trees again. I knew I wouldn't make it. I was fast, but with his stride in this short amount of distance, he would catch me in about three steps. I just stood there, not knowing what to do. He walked over to my side and opened the door. "Get. In."

Discretion being the better part of valor, I got in. While he made his way over to the driver's side, I started to freak out a bit. What if the Monster saw us? What if he came now?

"What are you doing here?" I blurted out as soon as he got in and closed the door.

"I could ask you the same thing. What are you doing out at two thirty in the morning, and why are you running when you've rolled your ankle?" He raised his eyebrows at me.

"I couldn't sleep and I wanted to run. My ankle is better. I can't use the treadmill without waking everybody up, so I thought it would be no big deal to go for a run right now. It's not like I expected to have someone outside my house watching me." I felt like an awful person. I was making him sound like a nutcase, but I needed the attention off me and onto him.

"What are you doing here, anyway?" I asked. "Are you stalking me?"

He wasn't even looking at me. He was staring out the side window scanning the street. For what, I could only guess. "Yes, Jasmine, *I'm* a stalker. You must be tired because your little act is slipping."

I pretended to sulk. Was I ever going to catch a break with him? Why didn't I fall for some nice, dumb jock who believed everything I said? Did I have to be attracted to an intelligent guy? So, I guess my sulk was kind of real. Why was nothing ever easy?

"What is it you think I'm doing, Easton?" Sometimes playing dumb is enough. I was pretty sure he wouldn't believe me, but his life was in danger if I didn't convince him.

He turned in his seat to face me. "I think you're doing something dangerous."

Oh boy. Not good. Underestimating him was a bad idea. "Dangerous? Running is dangerous? I know I rolled my ankle, and it's the middle of the night, but really?"

"Jasmine, I'm tired, I don't want to play this game anymore. Unless you want to tell me what's really going on, you should just go back in the house and go to bed." He sat back in his seat and stared out the windshield.

"I told you, I'm going for a run." I put my hand on the door handle, and his hand shot out and grabbed mine.

"No you don't. The only place you are running to is your front door."

"What are you talking about? I told you I came out here to run." I felt like having a temper tantrum. Like a real honest-to-goodness tantrum, right there. It was the outside of enough. I just couldn't deal with this too. He was so frustrating. I loved him, but he was going to ruin everything.

"Sugar, whatever is really going on, you have to stop it." He looked determined.

I realized at that moment that he hadn't bought my act at all. Not even a little bit. He might not know everything that was going on, but he was on the right road. How many nights had he sat out here? This was far more dangerous than I originally thought. I needed to get away from him and stay away until this was all over.

"Let go. I'm going back inside. I can't do this. I don't know why you're here. We're not together. Go home, Easton." He still had hold of my hand. I knew he could feel it shaking. I was glaring at him, but it didn't seem to be working.

He spoke as if he was choosing his words very carefully. "If you go anywhere but to your front door right now, I am going to wake your mother and tell her what I think you're doing. She'll never let you leave the house again."

I ripped my hand out of his and flung the door open. I got out, slammed the car door, and stomped all the way to my front door. By the time I got there, he had grabbed me and pulled me into a hug. No. No, no, no. I could not give in to him no matter how much I wanted to with every fiber of my being. He tilted my chin up and stared into my eyes like he was trying to figure something out.

"Jasmine, what are you doing? You have to let me help you."

I took a deep breath. "If you want to help me and yourself, you will go home." I wriggled out of his grasp and went inside without looking back. I really wanted to slam that door too, when I got in, but rationality prevailed, and I crept back to my room instead.

My life sucked.

Chapter 11

I was in English class when the text came in.

Take the number 4 bus to the rest stop off Hwy 10. Exit #97. I am sure I don't have to remind you what will happen to Lily if you disobey me. You have 1 hour.

I had been worried all morning about what happened last night, but it looked like the Monster wasn't aware of it. Instead, it was time to go. I got a jolt of fear when I read the text, and then peace. Strange. Maybe it was shock. Didn't matter at this point. I had to get moving. I asked Mrs. Thomas if I could go to the nurse. Instead, I went to my locker and stopped in the bathroom.

I had a few preparations to make. I used the toilet, then changed my clothes and shoes before I went out the side doors by the gym. I walked quickly to the bus stop three blocks over. I hoped no one had seen me, but after-school detention for skipping class didn't seem like that big of a deal at the moment.

I felt a little numb. I thought I would be shaky or scared, but really, I just felt calm. It was finally happening. The waiting was over. I was ready. I was putting my plan into action, and if I was lucky, the Monster would be caught.

I hopped on the public bus and opened up my phone to read the text one more time.

I texted Caedan to tell him I wouldn't be home this afternoon. I gave him the password to my username on the computer. Then I told him I had a mission for him.

When he was little, he loved to play spy. I used to set up missions for him. I would send him to find out what mom was making for dinner, but he had to do it without her seeing. He loved it. I knew, at first, he would think it was a game. Even though he was twelve, he wouldn't be able to resist. I warned him to follow my instructions exactly. I said a prayer that it would go off without a hitch. Unlikely, I knew, but it couldn't hurt to ask.

At some point—probably sooner rather than later—he would know it wasn't a game. I was trusting him to hold it together and follow my instructions. He had to activate the GPS, have the texts sent to his phone, make sure the e-mails got sent, and call 911. I knew it was a lot to ask of a twelve-year-old, but Caedan was the most capable member of my family. Even if he fell apart, there was enough information there. I know he would make sure the police got it. I was just praying it would work in my favor.

It made me sad and scared to think I may never see my family again. I knew what kind of pain my death or even disappearance would bring. We had lived it already once. If I could have thought of a better way to catch him, I would have. I hated that I might cause so much pain if it went wrong. I could feel the fear trying to get a foothold when I started to think about what I had to do. Time to stop thinking and start doing.

I spent the rest of the bus ride repacking my backpack and mentally reviewing my plan. I hadn't had time to test it as well as I would have liked, thanks to Easton's little interruption last night, so I was just going to hope it was as good as I thought it was. No more time to plan now. I had arrived.

As I stepped off the bus, I got my next set of instructions.

Sit on the bench next to the trees on the far side of the building. Walk slowly. Face forward.

That was simple. I could do that. My heart was starting to pound. All I could think about was how many holes there were in my plan and what could go wrong. I hated not knowing what was going to happen. I had a vivid imagination, and I had to force myself not to dwell on all the horrible things that could happen. One foot in front of the other. I needed to stay focused.

I hobbled slowly toward the bench and sat down. I was facing the highway and the building with all the restrooms, so I could see almost everything going on at the rest stop. This was a little strange. There were people everywhere. Why would he have me come here? There were truckers and families stopping here to use the restrooms. It wasn't packed like on a weekend, but it was a Friday afternoon, so it was fairly busy. I guess it made sense. He could watch and make sure I did what he said. I was right not to have called the police yet. He would have seen that coming and just walked away. I had thought about it, but I couldn't risk it. If he was watching, he would get away. Again.

I pulled out my phone and got to work.

I saw a newer-looking truck pull into the parking lot, and a man got out. He was tall, blond, and kind of muscular. He went into the restroom and came out again, talking to another guy. The man chuckled and moved on to his car. Blond guy turned and walked away from his truck and toward my bench. He stopped directly in front of me. He looked vaguely familiar.

"Excuse me, do you know how to get to Lake Charles from here?" He was smiling, but I couldn't see his eyes through the mirrored sunglasses he wore. I thought it was odd that he would ask me for directions. I was obviously not an adult. Not that he was that old. Maybe midtwenties. Why wouldn't he ask one of the other adults nearby? Was this a line?

"I'm sorry, I'm new here. I don't really know my way around yet." I smiled briefly and looked down at my phone, hoping to be dismissive but not rude.

"Well, that's okay, Jasmine. I'm new here too. I think we'll find our way where we're going just fine," he said as he stared down at me from where he stood, blocking my line of sight to the restrooms.

My head snapped up when he said my name, and my stomach felt like it hit the ground. How could this be him? He didn't look like I ever imagined the Monster to look. I thought he would be ugly, deformed, and awful. He was no Easton Ward, but he was so... normal.

I was completely taken off guard. I expected a repeat of the day of the meet. I expected to be grabbed from behind. How was he planning to get me to go with him? Oh, right. Same way he got me here. Lily. I would just go to his truck with him, and it would look like we were together. No one would be the wiser. Clever. Clever and really creepy.

Was this what he had done with Daisy? Had he threatened to take me? Had she gone without any fuss because she thought I was in danger? I couldn't believe how sick I felt in this moment. My sister had died at the evil hands of this man. I was shaking, and I felt cold sweat pour down my back. I didn't want to think of the horrible things he had done to her as he stood there smiling at me. I could feel bile in the back of my throat. I was angry and terrified both at the same time.

"So, Jasmine, we're just going to make our way over to my truck, and you are not going to draw attention to yourself in any way. You understand? Nod your head." He looked serious. I nodded and stood up. I felt like my feet were filled with lead, and my heart was pounding out of my chest. I limped as we made our way to the truck. He put his arm around me as we walked. I had to control myself not to shudder and gag. All I could think about was that those hands had killed my sister.

Before we got there, he took my backpack and my phone from me. He threw the backpack in the trash and set the phone behind the front tire of the truck. He opened the truck door and I climbed in. He closed and locked it. It was happening so fast.

I looked out the windshield. Everything looked so normal. I realized while I was sitting there that I had just done what I had told Lily I would never do. I got in this truck. I was taking a chance with my life, when I promised her I wouldn't. But if it kept this monster away from her, it was a promise worth breaking. All I could do was keep praying that what I had set in motion would work. Come on, Caedan, just follow the plan.

As he walked around to the driver's side, I had to mentally slap myself. I needed to be paying attention to my surroundings and to what was happening. No time to give in to the fact that he was making my skin crawl. I had a job to do.

He got into the car on his side. He smiled, and it reminded me of a snake.

"Jasmine, I want you to open the glove compartment and take out the plastic baggie inside." I opened the glove box. Inside was the baggie, but there were also zip ties and an ugly-looking knife. I did what he asked, while trying to keep my hands from shaking.

A piece of fabric that looked exactly like the last one was sitting ominously in the bag. "Open the baggie, but don't do anything else with it. I want you to lay your head on my shoulder." I must have looked like I was going to balk because he frowned. "Do it now, Jasmine." He had an edge to his voice that I remembered from when he grabbed me at the meet.

I slowly scooted over on the bench seat and laid my head on his shoulder. He put his arm around my shoulders.

"Now take the material out of the baggie, place it over your face, and breathe normally."

This time I couldn't keep my hands from shaking. This was the most scared I'd ever been. Even more than at the meet. He was so calm but so scary. I didn't want to do this. I couldn't be passed out and not know what was going on. I needed to stay in control and awake. I didn't want to be sick like last time. I needed to see what was going on.

I felt the tears start, and I couldn't see to get my hand in the bag. He looked angry.

"You were doing so well. Don't make me have to do this for you, Jasmine. You know you have no choice in this. I told you it was you or Lily. You agreed. Do it now, or I will be forced to do something I don't want to do." He squeezed my right shoulder hard. He obviously meant business.

"Can I please just close my eyes or something? Please?" I hated to beg, but if it kept me from having to breathe that stuff in, I would. "I got pretty sick from it last time," I sniffed and tried again to stop the tears. He reached up with the hand resting on my shoulder, grabbed my hair, and yanked my head back so I was looking him directly in the eyes. He started talking through his teeth.

"You are trying my patience. I thought you were going to make this easy. Do it now before I decide to make this much harder on you." He let go and looked away. He was tapping the steering wheel with his thumb.

"I have a schedule to keep and you are putting us behind."

Okay, there was no negotiating. I obviously didn't have a choice. Nodding, I slowly reached into the bag. I couldn't think of anything that was going to make this any better. I raised the material to my face and breathed shallow breaths. The sides of my vision started to go dark immediately. And then... nothing.

Chapter 12

When I awoke, my head was spinning again. It took me a few moments to orient to my surroundings. I tried to roll onto my side, but I was having trouble. I closed my eyes again for what could have been minutes or hours. I couldn't tell.

When I opened them again, the room wasn't spinning anymore, but I still felt like my eyelids weighed a ton. I looked down and confirmed that I was still wearing the same clothes. My shoes and ankle brace were still on. Thank you, Lord! Something was going right in this nightmare.

I tried to turn over again and realized my right hand was zip-tied to a bed frame. I reached into my brace with my left hand and pulled out the small knife I had hidden there and put it under my pillow. Obviously, the Monster didn't know I was left-handed, since he had zip-tied only my right. There was a knot in the pit of my stomach. I didn't even want to think about what would come next. Fear was trying to get a foothold, but I couldn't let it. Caedan should have followed my instructions by now.

Time to take an inventory of the room. It looked old and run-down, at first glance. Wood walls and floor. It was a loft of some kind. In front of the bed, a section of the wall opened to the floor below. I couldn't hear anything except water lapping against something. There was some natural light, but no windows that I could see. It looked like it must have been some kind of storage area. I could see the beginning of the staircase all the way across the room, and the rest of the room was empty. Not a thing in it, except for the bed I was on.

I turned my head to the left and gasped out loud. On the wall next to the bed was a huge collage of photos, and they were all of me. A magazine of my life: moving day in California, with my mom and the twins in Wal-Mart, the first day of school here, with the girls at lunch, running during cross-country practice, and with Easton at the Art Walk. I wanted to throw up. My stomach started to heave. I knew he had followed me, but this was a whole different thing. This was my whole life. Seeing it this way was so scary and intrusive. I had known he had been watching, but to know that during some of the happiest moments of my life I was being stalked put my balance completely off.

How was I going to face this alone? It made me sick to think Daisy went through this and was as scared or even more than I was right now. Tears pricked the back of my eyes. I didn't want to think about what he had done to her because I could be next. I needed to pull myself together. The only way this could work was if I didn't lose it.

I took a deep breath, shoved the fear into one of those very convenient compartments, and locked it down. No time for that now. Falling apart could come later. If there was a later.

I heard a door downstairs open and shut. Footsteps, cabinets opening and closing. Then someone was coming up the stairs. I started to sweat. I wasn't sure how ready I was for this confrontation. My plan A was to just wait it out as best I could and hopefully the cavalry would arrive without me having to do anything. My Plan B was a little more confrontational, and I hoped I wouldn't have to use it. He was, as it turned out, a pretty big guy. I knew that, so I had planned accordingly, but he definitely had an advantage.

His steps were heavy, and my heart seemed to pound harder with each one. I closed my eyes, hoping he would think I was still asleep.

"Jasmine." I cracked my eyelids to look through my lashes. He had brought a chair with him. He sat backward on it at the end of the bed. "I know you are awake. Don't make me prove it."

I opened my eyes and said nothing.

"There's my girl."

The sweat on my body turned cold. It was warm in the room, but I couldn't tell. He didn't have any expression. He'd had sunglasses on when we were in the truck so I hadn't gotten to see his eyes, but now I could tell there was nothing there. He had a knife in his hand and was just holding it where his arms crossed on the back of the chair.

He must have taken his shirt off because he was just wearing a sleeveless undershirt, and I could see he had a tattoo on his shoulder. It was a daisy. I don't know why it shocked me so much, but it did.

The shakes were unavoidable now. My whole body was shivering. He saw where I was looking and glanced at his shoulder.

"Like it? I thought it was an appropriate way to remember your sister. Even though it turned out that you are the one I really want. If I'd known then that you would turn out so beautiful, I would have just taken you. Daisy turned out to be… a disappointment." He wasn't even looking at me; he was looking at the pictures on the wall. "All that time I wasted on her, and you were really the one. I should have been more careful in choosing." He turned his head back to stare at me. "But I've got it right, now. How are you feeling?"

How was I feeling? Well, gosh, I don't know. Pretty good, what with being stalked and kidnapped by my sister's murderer. I guess I was doing okay. How was I supposed to answer that? He really was certifiable, but I needed to keep him talking.

"Where are we?"

"Far enough away so that we won't be found. That's all you need to know. The question is: Are you going to be a good girl and do what I tell you? Or are you going to disappoint me, the way Daisy did?"

"I don't know what you mean. How did she disappoint you?" I hated talking to him about my sister. It made me mad and gave me the creeps at the same time, but any information I got could help. Keeping him talking instead of acting was definitely better.

"She told me she would stay. She told me she would do what I said, and then she tried to run. She lied. I can't stand liars. She said she loved me and she left. I told her we were meant to be together. She agreed."

He was starting to get agitated. He stood and started to pace. His voice got louder.

"I explained it all to her. How I had seen her at the hospital. How I knew from the way she smiled at me that we were meant to be together. She always spoke to me when she came to the hospital to visit. I knew then that she was mine. But then she had to go and ruin everything. She ran away the minute she had the chance. Don't you see? I didn't have a choice. She lied to me. I didn't know what to do for a while. I was so confused. I had been so sure. And then I saw you on the news. I knew then. You were so angry. You were beautiful and strong and you said what you felt. You didn't lie. You always told the truth. You were actually the one. I watched you."

The fact that he had been so close to us and we missed it freaked me out. How did the police not catch him? He was right there. How did he get away with it? He worked at my mom's hospital? That's how he knew us? I didn't remember him. I hadn't talked to everyone there like Daisy had. I always just went to the gift shop or sat in a waiting room, reading, when we were there. But Daisy talked to everyone. She had planned on being a nurse, like my mom, but wanted to work with the NICU babies. He must have been one of the people she got to know there. Out of everyone, he picked us. Completely random and terrifying.

"All this time, I waited. When you all decided to move, it was perfect. A fresh start for us. I couldn't wait. And then we got here and that idiot got in the way. He almost ruined everything. I almost killed him just for that. But who could blame him for falling in love with you? You were irresistible. I knew you would be honest and do the right thing. I knew you would get rid of him when I told you to. You're a smart girl. Smarter than your sister. You saved his life, Jasmine. You should be proud. Now we are together, and everything is the way it should be. Don't you see?"

That stupid press conference had caused all of this. I never should have done it. Then, again, because of that press conference I was going to have the opportunity to catch him—one way or another. I know it sounds crazy. I didn't want to die, but I wasn't afraid of it either. I wanted him brought to justice more than I wanted to live with him walking around free to do this to someone else's life. If he was caught, Lily could stop being scared, Caedan could grow up knowing the Monster was in jail, and my mom could move on. Would it be better if I came out alive? Absolutely. But it wasn't the most important thing. My plan was not to guarantee I got out alive but that he got caught.

Please, Lord, he needs to get caught, or all of this will have been for nothing.

So far, so good… until he came and sat down on the bed next to me. He leaned over and ran his hand over my hair. He pulled out my ponytail holder and ran his fingers though my hair again and again, just staring at me. He had calmed down some and was smiling that creepy smile again that didn't match his eyes.

"I am so happy you're here. I have waited so long for you." He spoke almost like he was talking to someone else.

He had a look in his eye that I didn't like at all. My stomach started to roll. This was getting bad. I didn't allow myself to think about where he was going with this. Keeping that particular box locked down was critical. Time for a distraction.

"May I please go to the bathroom?" I really did have to go, and if it kept him off track, all the better. He sat up and looked at me.

"Jasmine, I want you to promise you are not going to try to get away once I undo this tie." He ran his hand up and down over my wrist. "I know we haven't had much time to get to know each other. You may not be ready to understand that I will never let you go. I do know you are an honest girl, and if you give me your promise, you will keep it."

Here is where this guy went so very wrong. I was a much better liar than my sister. I'm the sneaky second child. I have ways of getting away with things that Daisy could never have understood. Not only was I a good liar, I was pretty sure I had a gift for acting.

After Easton pointed out some of what I considered gifts and he considered flaws, I had thought seriously about it. I had been conning people my whole life. I really needed to pray about it when this was over because I probably enjoyed that a little too much. I tried not to use my powers for evil, but I have to say it's a good thing I know Jesus. I'm far from perfect. And I'm not sure why Easton was the only one who could see right through me, but for now I was thankful. At this moment, however, I wasn't going to try to get away. Building a little trust with this guy wasn't going to hurt my situation and would help me later. I needed to be sure I had given enough time for the plan to be executed. I was just going to stall and pray that everything went the way I had planned.

Lord, I know I have been lying, but please don't let him hurt anyone else.

I looked into his eyes and made it count. "Okay. I promise." Sincerity was everything in making someone believe.

He hesitated a moment. Then he reached over me to wedge the knife between my wrist and the zip tie. He popped it off with a flick of his wrist, and I was free. He pulled me up and led me across the room by my arm. I was a little nervous that I had left the knife under the pillow, but it wasn't all I had, and there was nothing I could do now.

As we started down the stairs, there was a crash outside.

He stopped and turned to me. "What have you done?"

I made my eyes go blank with innocence. I shook my head. "Nothing. I swear."

He had a hold of my upper arm and shook it hard. "Jasmine, I told you. I will take Lily. I will kill Caedan, your mother, and anyone else you care about if you have betrayed me. Who's out there?" he said through his teeth. The veins in his neck were protruding, and I was afraid this was it. He was going to snap.

"I don't know. I swear. I did exactly what you said. I left school. I did what you wanted."

He stared at me a moment. Then he nodded and started to drag me down the stairs. "I hope you are telling the truth or you just killed your family."

Once we got to the bottom floor I realized this wasn't a cabin. It was a boathouse. We were on a lake or a river. There was a roll-up door on one wall and a winch on the other end of the room. It was old and looked like there hadn't been a boat in here for a very long time.

There were chairs by a table, and he shoved me into one of them. "Stay there and don't move. I am going to see what's going on. If you try to get away, I will find you. Don't test me." He gave me a hard look and moved toward the door.

He went outside and I tried to decide what to do. What was happening? Could the police be here already? Could they have tracked me and figured it out yet?

I jumped out of my seat, ran up the stairs, and grabbed the knife from under the pillow. I was back in my seat with my knife back in my ankle brace in less than thirty seconds. Whew.

There was something going on outside. I heard what sounded like a scuffle, and something hit the outside wall of the boathouse hard. Then, some shouting. No. I was imagining things. Then the door opened, and Easton was shoved into the room and then jerked back against the Monster with the knife against his throat. I jumped out of the chair.

No! The bottom dropped out of my stomach. I wanted to scream. This was not the plan. He was not supposed to be anywhere near here. How did he find me? Did he follow me? Did Caedan call him?

Easton's mouth was dripping blood, and he looked roughed up a little. The Monster was not unscathed though. One eye was partially closed, and his shirt was covered in dirt like they had been rolling around on the ground.

"Well, look what we have here, Jasmine. Your boyfriend was trying to rescue you. Did you plan this together?"

I knew my reaction in this moment would either save or kill Easton. I had to make this the best acting job of my life. I looked the Monster right in the eye and gave it all I had.

"No. I don't know why he's here. I broke up with him. I told him to stay away from me. I told him I didn't like how he tried to run my life, and I wanted to be single. He's probably just jealous and followed me."

I refused to even look at Easton. I could not allow emotion to throw me off. "I don't like him anymore."

The Monster didn't look convinced. He was moving the knife at Easton's throat back and forth, not quite touching his skin.

"So if I kill him, you won't care?"

"I didn't say that. I said I don't like him anymore. I don't want him dead, but I don't want to be with him either. I don't want to be responsible for him dying. Can you just let him go? Or leave him here, and I'll go wherever you want." I wasn't begging, but it was getting close.

Easton looked shocked and then angry.

"No!" he shouted. "You are not going anywhere with him. Let her go, you psycho!" He started to struggle. I saw that the Monster wanted to slit his throat, but he kept looking at me as if wondering what I would think if he did it right in front of me. I had to do something. I couldn't let him die because of me. Because he loved me. I couldn't live with that.

"I will go wherever you want! Please, let's get out of here. Just you and me. You can leave him zip-tied to the chair. I already promised I wouldn't try to get away. Please, just leave him." I was begging now. I wanted his attention on me.

The Monster looked like he was trying to decide if I was lying.

"Okay. I am going to choose to believe you. You're going to have to show me you can be trusted. We have to leave anyway, since lover boy here probably called the cops." He shoved Easton into the chair I had been sitting in and handed the zip ties to me.

"Tie him to the chair tight. I will check them, so don't go easy."

I nodded. He grabbed Easton's hair and yanked his head back. He held the knife right under Easton's chin. "If you touch her, I will kill you, and then I'll come back for your brother and your cousin. Don't get cute."

"Let me up and we'll see who kills who." Easton growled and then spit in his face. I gasped as the Monster punched him hard in the stomach and Easton doubled over. I was trying not to cry. This had to stop. I had to get the Monster away from him. I was so scared he would kill him.

"Stop, please, stop. I hate fighting. It makes me sick." I was trembling all over.

The Monster looked over at me. He let go of Easton's hair and stepped back, wiping his face. "Get it done. Don't make me regret not killing him."

I stepped forward and bent down to secure his wrists to the arms of the chair. My hands were shaking, and I was having trouble getting the zip tie fastened. Easton was still doubled over in pain.

"Jasmine," Easton breathed into my ear as I leaned forward. "Don't go anywhere with him. He's going to kill you. I won't be able to protect you if you leave here."

I ignored him and moved to the other side. I could not afford a mistake at this point. His life was at risk. I finished with the second zip tie. I wished I could slip him the knife, but the Monster would see. As I stood up, I squeezed his hand. I hoped he would know I loved him. I wasn't sure now how this would end, so I hoped he knew I just couldn't live with being responsible for his death.

I walked over to the Monster and waited. He grabbed Easton's wrists and pulled. They were tight, I knew. The Monster shoved an old rag in his mouth and tied it with a bandana around his head.

Hopefully, with my plan, the police would find him and get him undone soon. I had been at this location long enough for them to check it out, once Caedan had logged onto the website. The battery in the GPS in my ankle brace still had a lot of hours left, and they should have tracked me here. Thankfully, the Monster had let me keep my brace on.

He grabbed my arm and started to pull me out the front door. My throat clenched shut. Sirens! As soon as the door opened, I heard them. Pretty far in the distance still, but they were there. Sirens. Really? A girl is kidnapped and they use sirens? Holy Cats, this was bad.

The Monster stiffened, and then looked enraged.

"Looks like your boyfriend did call the cops. Good thing I was prepared for a quick exit. He's not as smart as everyone thinks he is. We'll be long gone before they get here," he said as he yanked me by my arm.

He seemed to not need a response, so I kept quiet. He dragged me around the back of the boathouse. I was just thankful we were moving away from Easton. As he pulled me over to the dock, I realized there was a boat moored there. I looked around and saw that we were on one of Louisiana's swampy rivers. Lots of foliage on each side, and I couldn't see very far downstream. Lots of twists and turns. Not so great for rescue. My heart gave a leap in my chest. Would they still be able to find me?

He dragged me into the boat and zip-tied my left ankle to a metal support underneath the seat. Not comfortable. He started the motor and we took off. I could hear the sirens getting closer pretty fast, but I knew we would be lost down the river in no time. I hoped the GPS worked in a swamp.

We moved down the twists and turns of the river quickly. I was starting to look for a way out. We were away from Easton, and the police were already nearby. I needed to be sure they would still catch him. There were so many small inlets and channels veering off the river, I couldn't figure how anyone ever found their way out. The water looked murky and green. It looked like there could be all kinds of really disgusting stuff in that water. No way should I be thinking what I was thinking.

I couldn't hear the sirens anymore, just the boat. There didn't seem to be anyone else on this part of the river, and the sun was going down. All of this did not add up in my favor. We weren't very far downriver now, but the farther into the swamp we got, the harder it would be for them to find us. I could not let him escape this time. Drastic action needed to be taken.

I stood up.

His was livid. "Jasmine, sit down. You will turn us over," he said between clenched teeth.

Duh.

"Don't make me hurt you."

I shifted my weight from one foot to the other quickly. He couldn't reach me without letting go of the rudder. The boat had an outboard engine, so I needed to watch that, but otherwise, it was more dangerous for me in the boat.

"Jasmine, I mean it. Sit down!"

Time to go.

I threw myself to the side. He did exactly what I hoped, which was let go of the rudder to reach out to try to grab me. The boat did what physics said it should. It flipped over, and the Monster went flying. I hoped he would get ground up by the motor, but that was probably too much to ask for.

I held my breath as I went over. The water was warm and murky. I curled up and grabbed the seat for leverage. I popped my head inside the air pocket underneath the boat to catch my breath. I was really starting to panic that he would have the same idea, so I needed to be quick.

My heart pounded. I reached into my ankle brace and pulled out my knife. I cut the zip tie and pushed off to the side opposite where he went over. I stayed under as long as I could, swimming to what I hoped was the bank. I couldn't see anything in the slimy and sluggish water. I had to keep myself from thinking about what else was in there with me. I knew alligators were really common here. I was terrified of alligators. They give me nightmares. It was the one downside when I was doing my research to move here. I just needed to get myself out of the water. Now.

I came up and tried not to gasp for breath and make a ton of noise. I looked and the boat was upside down, floating down the river. There was no sign of him. I pulled myself up onto the slimy shore. It was humid and hot out. I felt like steam was coming off my body. I moved quickly for the trees. I thought they were mangroves by the way they sat low in the water and the big leaves, but I couldn't be sure. There were tons of flying bugs too. Good thing bugs didn't like me like they did my siblings. I kept moving.

I wanted him to follow, but not catch me. The trick was to keep moving along. It was getting harder to see, but I attempted to move toward what I thought was the direction of the boathouse. I stopped behind a tree every few minutes to see if I could see or hear him. He had to take the bait and follow, or all this would be for nothing.

I decided to stay in one place for a bit and check on what had survived my plunge into the swamp. My knife was in my ankle brace, safe and sound, and the GPS was still there too, taped around my ankle with duct tape. I hoped it had stayed dry. Waterproofing wasn't my first concern when I decided to tape it to my ankle, but I was pretty sure if it survived, the duct tape was why.

I pulled back the top of my shirt and reached into my bra. I could feel the packet in there. I pulled gently and it came out. Well, it looked mostly dry. I had packed some of Caedan's sneezing powder into a very small plastic baggie and taped it to the inside of my bra. I had been walking around like that for days. Hopefully I wouldn't have to use it.

I put two fingers of my left hand in the sneezing powder, closed it back up, and slipped it into my front pocket. When I'd gotten everything situated, I heard it. The sound was coming from my left. Someone was moving through the swamp toward me. Time to get moving.

I was going slowly now. There were shadows everywhere. Out of nowhere an arm shot out and grabbed me. I shrieked and a hand covered my mouth. It was him.

He pulled me to him and growled in my ear.

"You little liar. I thought I could trust you. You are just like her." He turned me to face him. He grabbed both my upper arms and squeezed. "Now I will have to take Lily. You have given me no choice." I kicked out at him, and he quickly moved his legs.

"Don't you dare touch Lily, you filthy creep. You have a choice. You choose to be evil. " I snarled at him. I had had enough. I was wet, slimy, dirty, and pissed off. I knew the police were out there. If I shouted to the high heavens now, they would find us. I was going to tell him what I thought. Enough with the games.

"You make me sick. You know why Daisy didn't love you? Why no one would ever love you? You are sick and disgusting. I hate you, and I hope when they catch you they kill you!" I was practically shrieking now. I was so angry. This demon had destroyed my family and all I wanted to do at that moment was strangle the life out of him.

I was breathing hard and waiting to see what he would do now. But he just smiled—which was the creepiest thing yet. Then he let go of one of my arms, reached out, and slapped me. Hard. My head snapped sideways, and I could taste blood in my mouth.

I tried to take a step back and fell hard to the ground, and he fell on top of me. Not good. I realized he had grabbed my shirt as I went down, and it had torn, straight down the middle. I tried to jab my hand with the sneezing powder in his face, but he grabbed both my wrists and held them over my head in one hand.

"You have caused me enough aggravation for one day, Jasmine. You need to learn to mind your manners."

I didn't want to panic, but now I was out-and-out terrified. I could tell by the look in his eyes I had pushed him over the line. He was crushing my wrists and pushing them into the ground. I tried to pull my wrists out, but he had a tight hold. He reached into his back pocket and pulled out another of those horrible zip ties, then secured it around my wrists. He looked down at what was left of my shirt. That creepy smile was back. He put his finger to my lips and drew a line downward to my chin and my throat.

I took a deep breath and started screaming like a banshee. I thrashed and kicked to try to throw him off me. This was not happening.

I heard a loud bellow coming from my left. Easton came charging out of the trees with Chase right behind him. Easton grabbed the Monster, threw him off me, and jumped on him. They rolled around on the ground pummeling each other.

I was screaming and scrambling to reach the knife in my ankle brace. I needed to do something. Chase bent down in front of me and grabbed it.

"Chase, you have to help Easton. Please take the knife. Go and help him." I was trying to catch my breath and not cry at the same time. Why wouldn't he just do what I said?

"I'm afraid I can't do that. Easton made me swear to stay with you no matter what. If I didn't agree, he would have left me behind." He looked over to where they were wrestling on the ground. He sounded calm, but I could see in his eyes he was worried. "My man has it under control. Let's just get you undone here."

Chase opened my knife and cut the zip tie. I was shaking and all I could think about was helping Easton. I stood up and started to move toward him. I couldn't just watch this happen. It was my fault. But Chase grabbed my arms and held tight.

"You have to stay here, out of the way. You'll only distract him and make it worse." Chase looked concerned. I saw a flash of metal and remembered the knife the Monster had been carrying. I felt Chase stiffen behind me, and I saw Easton and the Monster struggling over it.

"No!" I screamed and started thrashing against Chase's hold. I was trying to get loose, but he was much stronger than I was. I was crying and screaming for Chase to help him.

Easton had a hold of the Monster's hand that gripped the knife. As the Monster moved it forward, Easton twisted it and I heard a loud crack. The Monster dropped the knife and howled. Easton rolled on top of him, kicked the knife away with his foot, and started punching him in the face.

The Monster was trying to cover his face and was making wheezing sounds. I was still trying to get loose while Chase was trying to calm me down.

"Jasmine, breathe, darlin'. You have to calm down. He's gonna be all right."

From the direction of the river, I heard voices. The light was almost completely gone now. It was getting harder and harder to see.

"Jasmine, Easton. Where are you? Can you hear us? Chase, where are you?" I saw lights moving back and forth through the trees. It must have been the police, but the voices sounded familiar.

Chase yelled back and started moving toward the sound. "Over here! We're over here!"

Through the trees came Easton's dad, Reese, Chad, Trenton, and about ten police officers. When they saw what was happening, they all moved quickly. The police surrounded them with guns drawn.

Easton's dad pushed through the policemen. "Easton—stop, Son." Reese grabbed him under his arms and yanked him off. He was still struggling against his dad to get to the Monster.

"Easton, calm down. Shake it off." His dad turned him around to face him.

"Dad, he would have killed her."

"She's all right, Son. She's going to be okay." Reese had him by the shoulders and gave him a little shake.

"We got him."

Easton put his head down, blew out a breath hard, and nodded. When he looked up I saw that one side of his face was swollen, and there was blood coming out of his nose. It hit me then. I had come so close to losing everything today.

I started sobbing. He didn't die. The Monster was caught. Easton had saved me. This amazing guy who didn't even know me two months ago just risked his life to save mine. I couldn't believe how much I loved him. I didn't even know it was possible to feel like this about someone. It was like goose bumps and butterflies times a million.

He started to move toward me. . My breaths were coming in short gasps as I tried to pull myself together. Suddenly, it all seemed too much. I heard buzzing in my ears and everything started to tilt.

"Jasmine…" was all I heard before the darkness took over.

Chapter 13

When I opened my eyes, I felt warm and cozy. There was a gentle rocking motion and a hum of a motor. Where was I? I couldn't see much but noticed a light out ahead. It was so dark. I figured we were on the river. I could hear the water lapping against the side of the boat. There was a blanket around my shoulders. I breathed in Easton's smell and knew I was safe. He was here.

"Sleeping Beauty, I'm startin' to think you do this just to get my attention." I was sitting in Easton's lap. My head was resting on his shoulder, and he had his arms around my waist. "And you never wait for me to kiss you awake."

I tilted my head back to look up into his face. "Sorry about that."

He looked down and frowned. I followed his gaze and realized my shirt had gaped open down the front where the Monster had torn it. I tried to pull it together.

"Hold on." He reached behind his head and pulled his T-shirt off. He held it out to me. The problem was I was so busy staring at his chest that I didn't even notice him trying to give me his shirt. You know how, in the movies, when the gorgeous guy takes his shirt off and all the girls in the audience go crazy screaming? This was, like, a thousand times better. Why had I never seen him with his shirt off before?

"Uhh, Jasmine?"

"Hmmm?" I finally looked at his face.

"The shirt?" He wiggled it at me. I heard laughter from behind him. I could see that Chase, who was driving the boat, had his head turned away and his shoulders were shaking. Really? I narrowed my eyes at him when he snuck a glance at me. Hey, a girl couldn't help it if his hotness was extraordinary. Sheesh.

I took the shirt and pulled it over my head. I turned around to settle back against Easton again so I could actually speak.

"How did you find me?"

"Caedan. Once he figured out what was going on, he phoned me. I called 911 and we started tracking you. I left him at the road before the boathouse turnoff to wait for the police. He was spittin' mad, but I took his phone and found you.

"That is not what I wanted him to do. He wasn't supposed to call you."

"Yeah, I got that." He looked angry. I guess I should have felt a little guilty now that I had lied to him. Again. But all I really felt was bad that he had been dragged into it and so relieved that he wasn't hurt. "How did you find me so fast after we left the boathouse?"

"When we were tracking you, I saw you were right by the river. I called Chase to bring his boat and meet me there. You had been stationary for a while, and I was worried that he'd found the GPS and took you out on the water. When Chase got there, he found me tied to the chair." He scowled down at me.

"He had worked that gag out of his mouth and was makin' more noise than a hound sittin' on a nail." Chase laughed.

"Anyway"—he glared at Chase—"we launched the boat and came after you."

What an amazing family he had. They would just drop everything and come running without question. "Thanks for helping find me, Chase." I smiled at him.

"Anytime." He grinned. "I'm glad you're okay. I thought this one was going to come out of his skin." He nodded at Easton.

"How are you feeling?" Easton sounded serious.

"Better, now that I'm with you. I'm glad you're here. I'm normally afraid of the dark." Of course with him here I didn't have any fear or panic at all. I actually felt like I had just drunk a large coffee. I felt this buzz of happiness. Weird.

I could hear him huff. "You're kidding, right?"

"No, I'm not. The dark gives me panic attacks. Ever since, well, you know," I mumbled.

"Jasmine, how is it that you're afraid of the dark, but you will run off with a serial killer to whatever horrible plan he has for you without a blink of an eye? You didn't even hesitate. I love you, sugar, but you have to get your priorities straight." He was really angry.

"I do have them straight. I had to go with him, or he would have killed you and all the others. That's not the same thing. I didn't have a choice."

"Jasmine, you always have a choice, and you chose not to trust me. I'm still so angry at you. You could have been killed. You went into this thing by yourself. You put yourself in danger. Why didn't you go to the police? You could have asked for my help."

I had turned around to sit sideways so I could see him. "No, I couldn't. You wouldn't have understood. I couldn't risk any of you. He threatened to kill you, Trenton, and Chase if I ever spoke to you again. He grabbed me off the road during the meet. He threatened all of you and my family—"

He broke in before I could say more. "You didn't trust me to help you. You obviously didn't think I could handle it. You lied to me, again. And you broke your word. I thought he was going to kill you. How do you think it was to be left tied to that chair knowing all the horrible things he could do to you?" He looked beyond furious.

"I'm sorry you are so mad. I know I broke my promise, but he was going to take Lily. The police couldn't catch him last time, and here they didn't even have any information about him like they did in California. What did you think would happen? They had to catch him in the act. He's totally capable of killing. We know that already. He almost killed you today. I couldn't live with that. No way. So go ahead and be mad. I wouldn't change it."

I tried to get up off his lap. He pulled me back down.

He took a deep breath and sighed "Now, sugar, don't go gettin' all worked up. We obviously have some things to work out. Did you even hear the part where I said I love you?" He was rubbing my arms.

"I may have." I felt a smile coming on. How did he do that? Turn everything around and make me smile?

"And you have nothing to say back to me?"

"Well, I guess I love you too."

He leaned in and kissed me. It would have been perfect if it had just been the two of us, but it was still a beautiful thing.

On the way back I filled him in on what I had planned. I had purchased online, with my mother's emergency credit card, a pretty sophisticated GPS tracking device that would track me just about anywhere. It used satellite technology, and I could be tracked from a website when logged on. It also had the capability to send text messages every few minutes with notification of my location to a designated number. I told Caedan I needed him to activate it from home and use his phone to track me.

I had also typed up an e-mail to a prominent homicide detective in the area, giving all the information I had collected on Daisy's case and everything that had happened since we arrived. It also detailed what I had planned. I used an application that allowed me to schedule e-mails to be sent out by a certain time every day. If I didn't get home to shut it down, the e-mails would go out. Mr. Thatcher, Coach Anderson, and Mrs. Connolly were also to receive a copy.

Just in case, I sent pictures by text to Caedan of the rest stop, everyone there, and every car in it, while I had been sitting there waiting. I had even gotten a pretty good one of the Monster sent off before he ran over my phone. I had tried to cover all my bases. I thought I had done everything I could to help them find me and catch him. I expected Caedan wouldn't follow the plan exactly, but calling Easton was not on my list of things I thought he would do.

I knew we must be getting close to the boathouse, but we were moving very slowly since travel on the river was difficult in the dark.

"Are you ready for what's waiting when we get back?"

I knew what was waiting. I could imagine. Police and news vans everywhere. Microphones and cameras shoved in our faces. I got the creeps just thinking about it.

"Uhh… no. Can we just stay here, floating on the river, and never go back?"

He looked around and down into the water. "Hmm… nice as that sounds, I'm not really a fan of the swamp."

"It's really not too bad. I'm not saying I want to build a summer home here," I joked, and he gave me a squeeze.

As we moved down the river I thought about Daisy. We had caught her killer. The closure my family and I had been waiting for all this time had arrived. And while it didn't bring my sister back, I hoped it would bring peace and healing to my family. I hoped we could move on with the good memories and know that he couldn't ever hurt anyone else.

When we pulled up to the dock at the boathouse, there were police cars, fire trucks, and paramedics everywhere. I didn't see any news vans yet, but they couldn't be far off. When we got out of the boat, we were swarmed by Easton's family. They had apparently come down to help with the search. Once Easton found out what was happening, he had called his dad and the word went out. They were all there. I hadn't meant for all these people to get involved, but it was too late to be embarrassed. I was so grateful no one had been hurt.

I saw the police pull up to the dock in another boat. The Monster was sitting hunched over in handcuffs in the back. The police got him out of the boat, and everyone silently made a path for them to lead him through. He stood tall as if we were all watching a parade in his honor. Easton drew me back and put his arm around my shoulders. As they walked him by me, I looked him right in the eye. He gave me that creepy grin and spoke.

"This isn't over, Jasmine. It's just starting. You belong to me." He looked at Easton with a condescending smile. The policeman behind him shoved him forward.

I shivered and Easton squeezed my shoulder.

"Don't listen to him, sugar." Easton hugged me and whispered in my ear.

I nodded.

We got him, and that was all that mattered. He would have no more power over me, my family, or anybody I cared about. He was going to get what he deserved. Even though it could never be enough.

Easton was surrounded by his family when I made my way through the throng of people gathered at the end of the dock, I could hear yelling from one of the police cars parked up by the boathouse. It was rocking back and forth.

"Let me out, you jerks! I haven't done anything wrong. Let me out of here. I need to find my sister! You can't keep me here! I have to find her! Let me out!"

Caedan. What was going on? I ran up to the police car. One of the officers stopped me.

"Ma'am, we're just keeping him there until he calms down. He's been trying to sneak off and interfere with our investigation. It's for his own good."

I had never heard Caedan kick up a fuss like that.

"Well, I *am* your investigation. Can you please let him out now? He's just worried about me." I leaned down and looked into the window. They actually had him handcuffed to the back of the seat like a criminal. Holy Cow. What had he done?

"Caedan! Stop it! I'm okay. I'm here. They're going to let you out now. Calm down."

He looked at me through the window. His eyes got really big, and he just burst into sobs.

Oh my gosh! No.

"Open this door! Open this door right now!" I was pulling on the door handle, but it wouldn't open. "I need to get in!"

The officer opened the door, and I slid into the backseat and grabbed him. "Caedan, it's okay. I'm okay. I'm sorry. Are you all right?" I hugged him hard, and I couldn't stop the tears.

I hadn't realized until this moment how much I had been resigned to never making it back. I knew exactly how he felt right now. We had been here before. We were going to be okay this time, but it had been a close thing. He was trying to pull it together.

"Jas, what were you thinking? I thought he was going to kill you." He was wiping his face on his arm. "Are you insane? Easton is going to let you have it—if there's anything left when Mom's done with you."

Well, so much for our touching little moment. Of course, I knew he was just having trouble processing his emotions. He was the best little brother on the planet. If it hadn't been for him, I might not have made it out alive.

Then, from behind me, I heard one of my favorite sounds ever.

"Well, besides being grounded for the rest of her life, there will be enough of her left to be doing chores for ten kids."

And there she was. I slid out of the backseat of the police car and threw myself into my mother's arms. I didn't care how long she grounded me for. She could be mad for the rest of my life. I was just so happy to see her. I was sure I was the worst daughter in the world to put her through this a second time.

"Mom, I'm so sorry." I was sobbing into her neck.

She grabbed me and held on. Tears were streaming down her face. I thought about what she must have been feeling before she knew I was okay. She was taking big gulping breaths and squeezing me so tight.

"Don't you ever do that again. Don't you ever risk your life like that. What would I do, Jasmine? What would I do if something happened to you too?"

I knew she was right, but I was right too.

"I had to, Mom. I couldn't let him do that to someone else. It was the only way. I'm sorry. You weren't supposed to find out until after." I wasn't going to tell her right now that he had threatened to take Lily. Not right here. Maybe later. If I had to.

"Where's Lily?" I was trying to stop crying but it wasn't working.

"She's at Abigail's. We haven't told her." My mom was sniffling and looking for a tissue. Then she stopped and looked me right in the eye. Did I detect a slight gleam? Uh-oh. "I wouldn't want to be you when you have to explain to your sister exactly what you thought you were doing with this whole scheme of yours."

Ahhh. There's the Rose Rourke I know and love. Yes, a love for retribution runs in our family. I didn't really want to be me right now either. For many reasons. Sigh.

A police officer, this one in a suit, interrupted, "Mrs. Rourke?"

"Yes?" My mom was wiping her eyes.

"We're going to need to have Jasmine come down to the station to make a statement."

"I saw them bringing that man out. I know him from California. He worked at the hospital," my mom explained.

"Yes ma'am. Ellis Reed."

"Yes, that's him." My mom looked stunned.

"He also worked here at the high school as a custodian."

Well that explained a lot.

Easton had finally gotten free from his family that had been surrounding him and was walking up, when the officer spoke to him too.

"Mr. Ward, you're going to have to come also. There's a lot to go over, and we want to be sure we can put him away for a long time."

"Yes sir. I'll be there." Easton looked determined. "Whatever you need."

The policeman thanked us and walked away. Was this it? How could it be over so fast? We had caught the Monster. He couldn't add even one more picture to that horrible wall of photos. He had stolen so much from me and my family: my sister, my confidence, and two years of my life. He had almost ruined us, but we had made it. Well, most of us.

I felt so strange. Shaky and lightheaded. But I also felt relieved and lighter. I knew we had a long road of healing ahead, but I had my family, and I had Easton. The Monster couldn't hurt us anymore.

I could breathe.

Epilogue

We sat on the end of the dock watching the sunset. Easton's family had decided to have a nobody-died-so-we-have-an-excuse-to-have-a-party party. Easton said his family uses any excuse to have a get-together. They were Southern. That's how it works. It seemed strange to me, but what can you do? They did help save my life.

We had snuck away after dinner to the pond. I sat quietly while he read what I had written to him. I had told Easton that my grand plan had included letters to each of my family members and him, in case I didn't make it. I knew it was morbid, but I wanted them to know how much I loved them and that I had made a conscious choice to risk my life. I was not a victim. I just needed to catch Daisy's killer. He couldn't be allowed to go free after what he did. He could not be allowed to torture my family anymore.

The last few days had been a whirlwind of media and police interviews. We had had to do a press conference. It was almost as horrible as the last time. The only thing that made it easier was that Easton was with me. We were finally on the downhill side of the media hype. It was over faster this time because, for one thing, I didn't die, and two, we caught him. It was only so interesting to the press when a story had a happy ending.

I did have a pretty stern interview with that homicide detective I sent the e-mail to. He was furious and stunned that I had taken it upon myself to do this thing. He told me all about the Monster. Ellis Reed had been in the foster system since he was five years old. He had been abandoned by his mother and had been passed from foster family to foster family, neglected and abused until he was sixteen. He got a job working in the maintenance department at the hospital. His mother's name was Dahlia. The police thought the flower names were the reason he was drawn to us. He had been obsessed with his mother and finding her again. When he found out she had died, he shifted his obsession to Daisy and then to me.

When we moved here, he moved also. He got a job working for the school, doing maintenance. He had access to all areas of the school, which was what made the stalking so easy. He could get into personal information, locker combinations, phone numbers. All of that stuff was in the files at school. He was there many times after hours. No one even thought it suspicious. He had no criminal record—not even a parking ticket—so he passed all the criteria to work at the school.

The detective explained to me in excruciating detail what could have happened to me and how lucky I really was. I told him I didn't believe in luck. I believed in doing the right thing and praying a lot. His answer to that was, "The Good Lord looks after fools and children." Good thing I'm still a minor or I might have been offended.

I had come such a long way since we moved here. I felt like I had become the girl I had been meant to be before Daisy's murder. I felt comfortable in my own skin again. I wasn't afraid anymore. I had stood up for my sister, my family, and myself. I didn't have to live my life in fear. I was looking forward to my life in Lafayette. I hoped Easton could get past the fact that I had lied to him. I hoped he loved me enough and thought I was worth it. It was the only thing I had left to worry about. Could he forgive me?

During the last few days Easton and I had had zero time alone together. They interviewed us separately, and with everything going on, we hadn't even had time to talk on the phone except to say good night. I was pretty sure that he wanted to yell at me in person anyway, so here we were.

Easton put the letter down and stared out at the water. He had been quiet for a long time, when he finally turned to me. He was still upset—I could tell.

"Jasmine, you're going to have to promise me that you won't ever be this stupid again."

"Umm, Okay. I promise." I smiled.

"And no more lying to me. Not ever. Got it?" He looked very serious.

My smile got bigger. "Got it." I tried to look serious. It didn't work. I was just so happy to be with him.

"If it happened again. Right now. What would you do?"

My face went blank. Hmmm... What would I do? "I would tell you?" I hedged.

"Okay, I guess I am going to have to believe you."

I nodded. My smile was back.

"You said some pretty nice things about me in this letter." The corners of his mouth twitched.

"I guess I did."

"Did you mean them?"

"I guess so."

"You changed my life too. I love you, Jasmine." He leaned in and kissed me.

Now I felt like a normal sixteen-year-old.

THE END

About the Author

Elena lives and writes in a suburb north of Los Angeles. She has never lived anywhere besides California which is probably a good thing since she hates being cold and is terrified to drive in the snow. She loves being a wife and a mother to her three kids and three dogs, although really the bulldog is the fourth child who has never matured beyond the toddler stage.

A self proclaimed nerd, she has been writing since she was a child. She has only recently, however, come out of the closet about this to her family and friends. They now understand better, but not completely, why she talks about characters in stories as if they are real people.

Website: Elenadillon.com

Twitter: @ElenaDillon

Facebook: ElenaDillonAuthor

Made in the USA
Charleston, SC
02 July 2014